Too Cold for the Weather

By

Sarah Kressy Giliberti

Acknowledgments

There are many people I wish to thank, beginning with the mentors—from physicians to patients--who have taught me what I know about health care. In addition to these people, I thank Ed Kressy, who provided valuable support; without it, this work never would have reached completion. Patricia White's encouragement and editorial support were essential to create a polished result. John French created the cover, and I appreciate the outstanding technical support. Lastly I wish to thank my husband and son, who have taught me about patience, commitment, and above all love.

All characters represented in this novel are entirely fictitious. Any resemblance to persons either living or dead is purely coincidental.

To laugh often and much, to win the respect of intelligent people and the affection of children, to earn the appreciation of honest critics and endure the betrayal of false friends, to appreciate beauty, to find the best in others, to leave the world a bit better, whether by a healthy child, a garden patch . . .to know even one life has breathed easier because you have lived. This is to have succeeded!--R.W. Emerson

1.

October, 1995

At first the night's too dark to see through. Rosie lightly holds

the railing of the balcony and stands perfectly still. Her eyes stretch wide

but feel closed. She blinks and sees darkness followed by darkness that

spirals up and down and out of her. Shadows begin to take shape and

distinguish themselves from the night sky that is scattered with quickly

moving clouds. Trees. Deciduous and evergreen. It's fall in Maine. The

air is unusually warm for this time of year, but carries a hint of cold, warning of the season to come. There's a slight breeze and she senses the leaves falling. In the dark she can imagine the red, orange, and yellow leaves twisting through the air to find the ground where they will decay in the winter and the months that follow. The thick smell sweeps up and surrounds her and she thinks, "I am smelling death." It is with this thought that she quietly begins to cry. The rush of grief and sorrow she didn't have at the funeral, when she shook both his parent's hands, and later when she watched his ashes fly into the Atlantic ocean, and before when she held his hand and he smiled and said to her, "well, everyone has to go sometime, right?" Her knees bend to the ground and she lets go of the balcony railing to cover her face and weep. The raw concrete presses into her knees. After several minutes of memories she uncovers her eyes and looks again across the night. The clouds have moved and there's a sliver of moon now visible. No stars are shining but there is the moon. He had recited to her all she would have once he was gone. How the earth would turn and the flowers would bloom in spring. He told her to drink in the aroma of lilacs for him and wild lilies in the wet woods. He told her the moon would look the same. She turns and walks back into the room. It's not the same, she thinks, and shudders when the door slams shut.

It's the next morning. She opens her eyes and sees blue sky through the heavy curtains which look eternally stuck in night. She blinks as her eyes adjust to that sliver of light. Lying still, on her side, she's unable to remember a single dream. Odd. She always remembers at least some of her nighttime unconscious creations. The ceremony didn't need to be so far north in Maine. His wishes were to scatter his ashes in the Atlantic, but his parents had taken advantage of the sympathy of family and friends and decided upon a location far away from Boston, his last residence. After his initial reaction to his diagnosis, he had risen with equanimity and strength, and had started a support group for people living with AIDS. Not surprisingly, he'd become a leader in the community. To no surprise, the members of that group were not well enough to travel far. Lost in thought, she stares at the bright strip of sky and jumps at the knock at the door. Art, she thinks, and pushes off the covers to get to the entrance of her room. "Morning, sunshine!" he exclaims, striding in as she smirks sarcastically at his back. His pale brown hair, as usual, is too long for such a short cut, and undecided upon which way to grow. She creeps back under the covers as he takes a seat in the corner. He holds a steaming cup of coffee and slurps it in a way that makes her laugh. She hates it that he can cheer her up when she's determined to be miserable.

"Did you sleep?" he asks.

"A little." She's conscious of her uncombed hair and the tank top and short shorts she's slept in. He's like my brother, she reminds herself as her hands feel clammy. A drop of sweat rolls down her side. She sits on the bed, the covers over her feet, and hugs a pillow. "You?"

"Yeah, kind of, I guess." His brows furrow as he states, "I kept thinking of what his mother said."

"The renunciation?"

"Yup. That one. I mean, I'm not gay, and I have nothing against those who are, but . . . .. Did he say anything like that to you?" His mother had proudly told them how her son, near death, apologized for his gay lifestyle. She spoke of it as if he had absolved himself of a sin he had committed.

"He said how cute the nurse was, but that was early on."

"Male?"

She laughs. "Male."

"Maybe he did. She was the one with him at the very end." Rosie raises her eyebrows at him, then shrugs. "Anything's possible," she says. There is silence as they both retreat into thought and memory.

"What was it that he had told you after he was diagnosed? Remember?"

Rosie laughs. "Yeah. Born again virgin." Art laughs into his coffee, then tilts the cup toward him. His jeans are faded, with rips in both knees, and his T-shirt collar is stretched out. He looks unwashed but somehow clean. "You know, you're missing the breakfast of champions down there."

"Am I?" she asks.

"Unh hunh. Probably all cold and stale now."

"Shut up!" She laughs, sailing a pillow in his direction. She never did have good aim, she realizes, as it meekly falls into the curtain. "So do you still want to hike today?" she asks him.

"Yeah, that would be great. I was looking at the map and, you know, Acadia isn't all that far from here. Want to hit one of those trails?"

"Sounds good to me. I've only been there once, and it's beautiful."

Art stands and moves to the door. "All right, Rosie sunshine, you get yourself ready and I'll meet you downstairs."

"Right," she says as he closes the door behind him.

In the shower, she starts to think of when they met. In a windowless room in a hotel in Virginia, they gathered for their Peace

Corps training. "Look around you," they were told. "This is your new family. These are your new best friends." It was five years ago. She feels as though she'd known him forever. There were 32 in their group. She had been twenty-four at the time, and, looking around, noticed she was one of five twenty-something women, seemingly unattached. She guessed there was an equal number of young men in a similar situation. Her eyes traveled around the room, seeing Art with his then wife Bridget, and noting they didn't really fit with one another. He was tall and thin and she was short and busty with a look that made one sure she would eventually be heavy. It wasn't her physique, it was that she had the air of a person who doesn't like discomfort or to obey the word "no." Art also looked as though he didn't like this word, but his was more an air of defiance than a result of pampering. He looked thoughtful, and as if he could appreciate hard work. There were two other couples who appeared to be about 50. An older man with shaggy grey hair and an unruly mustache reclined in the back of the room, completely absorbed in doodling in his notebook and looking as if this were a brief stop in the developed world before moving on. Then she saw Octavius.

He was sitting in the front, but he was so animated in conversation that he appeared to dance. His hands fluttered around him as he spoke, then retreated to balance his chin as he listened. Although everyone was talking and the room was full of noise, his laughter dominated and somehow lent order to the cacophony. His grin caused deep crevices and well-worn lines around his eyes. He and one of the married, middle-aged women were engaged in conversation, and she watched as the woman first smiled politely, then turned her body toward him, uncrossed her arms, and began to smile with sincerity. It was amazing, Rosie thought, to see how she opened like a flower and took him into her confidence. He had black hair and grey-green eyes under black-rimmed glasses, simple but elegant, and certainly not cheap. Nothing about him looked cheap; his intricately patterned shirt, jeans, shoes, and thin gold necklace all looked carefully chosen, neatly put together. He had a solid build but delicate looking hands with long tapered fingers. His skin looked weathered, but he didn't appear that old. Maybe early 30's, she thought. She would learn that he could look almost any age. Sometimes his eyes would look like those of a child and at other times, ancient, as if they had witnessed the beginning of time.

She turns the water off and squeezes extra water from her curly brown hair. Has it only been five years? she wonders. Didn't I know him before?

She meets Art in the lobby of the hotel and they check out together. They'll drive back to Boston later, and he'll fly back to Colorado tomorrow. They load up the rental car and head north, to Acadia. Art drives, and Rosie enjoys gazing out the window and not thinking, for at least some of the drive.

"This is for you," Art says, and hands her a roll of toilet paper.

She laughs. It's an old Peace Corps joke. If you're going to stay with someone, you're always welcome as long as you bring an extra roll of toilet paper. "You didn't get this from the hotel, did you?"

"I did," he says, and looks over at her and grins. "Are you sure your room mate doesn't mind my sleeping on the couch?"

"Eh, she probably won't even notice. She usually works a double shift on Sundays, anyway. She'll come in at about midnight, or later, and be asleep when you leave."

He nods. "She's a nurse, right?"

"Yeah. I met her in the hospital, and I was there so often I sort of got to know her. She happened to be looking for a roommate when I was looking for a place, so . . ." her voice trails off.

"Timing." Art says. They are silent for a few minutes, listening to the sound of the engine and the noise from the radio.

"So what's she like?" Rosie asks.

"Jenny?"

"Is that her name? Your new squeeze?"

"Yeah. My 'squeeze' is a pretty cool lady. She's really smart, funny, kind of opinionated."

"What does she look like?"

He furrows his brows. "Why does that matter?" He always made a fuss out of appearances not meaning anything.

"Just want to get a visual."

"She's tall, kind of thin, I guess. She has long brown hair and brown eyes. She has this fantastic smile . . .." Rosie looks at him and watches the smile widen across his face as he talks.

"I'm happy for you, Art. It's about time you met someone. You deserve happiness, you know."

"Thank you." He glances at her, suspiciously, waiting for the sarcasm.

"Really!" She says.

The drive isn't long, and for the remainder of the trip, they don't really say much. They consult the map now and then, and she follows along with her finger, marking the towns as they pass. The beauty of Maine here is striking, and she's reminded that if the farthest north you travel is Kennebunkport, you really haven't visited this glorious, wild, and rugged state. There are times when she catches glimpses of the Atlantic's radiant blue, but the sea doesn't enthrall her a much as the forest. The leaves are firey orange and yellow, with many of the reds already on the ground. Evergreens peak out amongst the colors, and provide contrast, increasing the vividness. The sky is still blue, but she sees more clouds now. It's a perfect day, she thinks, and this makes her angry. She wants to mourn and to cry, but she can't in the presence of this beauty. In the middle of the anger she realizes that the view from the window pulses with Octavius' spirit: vibrant, colorful, and alive. He was more alive than most people dare to be. What she sees begins to turn into a feeling, and what she feels is spirit, his spirit spreading out first across the shore where they scattered him, now in the low hills, and eventually, out into the universe. This sensation warms her. She sighs and relaxes, letting go of the anger as she has so many times, and enjoying the sunlight that falls across her lap.

"You okay?"

"Yeah. Enjoying the view."

They step out of the car at the same time and walk over to a trail map with information about the park. The parking lot is gravel, surrounded by trees. There are few noises, and a light breeze comes and goes. Information about the park is tacked beneath glass under a wooden, roofed structure. They choose a fairly short trail which will take them to a highpoint overlooking the hills and the ocean. As they begin, their conversation meanders, not really settling on anything important. Their words are like a trickling brook, not finding places to pool. It is a relief for Rosie. When the trail begins to climb upward, they cease talking altogether. Art is used to altitude and doesn't break his pace or even breathe harder with effort. His long legs quickly increase the distance between them. He is a little ahead of her now, but she is unconcerned because the trail is well worn, and every now and then, he pauses to make sure she's still following.

This is the part of hiking she enjoys: the solitude with security. She feels alone, yet accompanied, and this state allows her mind to wander into crevices she's had to avoid, ignore, or even abandon. While her feet rhythmically fall one behind the other on damp soil, rock, and fallen leaves which color the ground, she daydreams. She sees the colors on the ground and the trees and granite rocks and boulders around her with her eyes, but in her mind, she's overseas again.

It had been an experimental program for the Peace Corps. Because the country to which they were assigned had a high early termination rate, the organization had begun a partnership program.

Instead of individual assignments, the sites took two volunteers at once. The intention was that everyone would have the support of another volunteer. Her partner was Octavius, and at first, when she learned he was gay, she was disappointed. She had hoped for one of the cute single guys, since the arrangement would provide such intimacy. But Octavius had a way of making friends, and he quickly felt like one of the best friends she had ever had.

They were assigned to a school where she would teach basic biology and he would teach English. Not to anyone's surprise, the students immediately loved him. His fourth graders surrounded him as soon as he walked in the door, jumping up and down and clamoring for his attention. He brought something every day for these children, and gave one child a treasure. With ritual-like intention, he handed them simple things, such as an unusually shaped stone, an original origami creation, or even a paperclip sculpture he had fashioned at home. There weren't many in his class, so he could easily keep track of who had gotten what and who was next to receive an item.

Rosie had had a harder time becoming loved by her students, who were a few years older. As she remembers, she humbly concluded that if she left the classroom feeling tolerated she had succeeded. She and Octavius got into the habit of meeting at the local bar every day after work. Most often, she would complain about her fifth and sixth grade students' misbehaving and not completing their assignments. They would fail her tests so miserably, that she didn't know how to create a sliding scale so that anyone would pass. Octavius listened, sipped a beer, worked on a paperclip, and offered suggestions. He brainstormed with her on how to make the learning fun, and how she could present it in a way applicable to their daily lives. She learned how to incorporate biology into their experiential world, and how to coax her students to have interest in her subject.

About a year into their assignment he began to tire. He couldn't meet her after school because he was exhausted. Instead of getting up early to work out, coming to school, meeting with her, then staying up late to write letters and grade papers, he slept late, went to school, and came home to sleep again after completing a minimum of grading. She discovered this when he had to take a taxi to school, since he'd missed the bus by oversleeping. It wasn't far, and she was surprised that he hadn't walked the path which provided a short cut. They sometimes did this together, to avoid facing the crowded bus. She noticed circles under his eyes, and, for the first time, his smile looked forced. He began to have a dry hacking cough which left his chest heaving and him gasping for air. She met him on the bus one morning and he had been forced to run a block not to miss it. He looked as though he had sprinted a mile.

"You okay?" she had asked.

"I . . .can't . . . seem to . . .catch my . . .breath." He gasped. His face looked pale and someone got up to give him a seat. "Thank you." He sat down gratefully and put his head between his knees. She stood next to him and touched his back.

"My god, Octavius," she said. He looked up and she touched his forehead. "You're burning up!"

When they got to school, she used the phone to call the Peace Corps main office. She waited with Octavius for the van to arrive.

"Probably just walking pneumonia. All those kids, you never know what we're exposed to." He laughed when she said this, and for a few minutes, she really believed that was all it was.

He didn't return that night, or the following week. She called the office and learned he was medically evacuated and would be evaluated further in the States. Her in-between-the-lines questioning couldn't bring her any more answers, and she hung up feeling anxious. She also felt lost. Without him, her days were mundane and dreary. Somehow the colors dulled and the dust from the roads seemed thicker. Everywhere she looked, she felt she was looking through a haze.

A month later she saw him emerge from a crowded bus and start walking up the hill to his house. She was shocked that she almost didn't recognize him, and if he hadn't been the only white person in a sea of dark-skinned Africans, she may not have noticed him at all.

"Octavius!!" She ran after him, waving her arms, although she knew it was unnecessary. For the same reason he stood out, she would, too. He turned and stopped to wait for her. She rushed up to him and hugged him, feeling bone where there had previously been muscle. She stepped away and looked at him, unable to hide her concern and confusion. Still, she smiled broadly and said, "Welcome home!"

"Thanks," he said. "But I'm just here to get my things, go in, and say good-bye to the kids."

"What? You're better now, aren't you?"

"For now." His eyes began to water up. "Shit, Rosie. Come on, let's not have this conversation here."

They walked to his house, and she was surprised at how slowly he moved, and how he still seemed to have some trouble catching his breath. They sat down on his balcony and she waited in silence for him to speak. She could hear dogs barking, the sound of a bus driving up the hill, and, farther away, children playing. When she could no longer bear it, she asked him, "So, was it pneumonia?"

"Yeah," he sighed and looked at his hands. "It was a kind of pneumonia."

"What kind?" It didn't make sense. If was something endemic to their country, couldn't he have been treated here?

"It's called PCP." He wouldn't look at her. Her confusion grew. She'd heard of it, but couldn't place where or when.

"And you got treated for it?"

"Uh hunh."

"So can't you just come back?" She felt stupid and naïve, as if she were one of the children in his class.

"Rosie." He looked at her. "I have AIDS."

Her hands went to her face and she watched his eyes well up with tears which then fell down his face. She didn't know what to think or say or feel and was horrified that her first thought was, how did he get it? She knew something about AIDS from her studies, but she wasn't entirely sure what it was or how she could get it. When she graduated with her degree in microbiology, AIDS was still rumored to be the "gay cancer." Could she touch his hand? Could she hug him? What about kissing him on the cheek? And then she looked at him, sitting there, hunching over, a portion of what he had been just a few months ago. His shoulders looked bony and his face looked thin. His glasses looked huge on his face, and his clothes wrinkled. She suddenly felt all he felt: the horror, the shame, and the loss. Her instinct for caring and nurturing overwhelmed her.

Standing up, she walked over to him, telling the scared useless voices to shut up. She wrapped her arms around him and held him.

"It's okay, Octavius. Somehow it will be okay." He bent his head, shaking it "no," and his shoulders began to heave with sobs.

The light dimmed. He told her what he had gone through to be allowed to come back. He said there was no medication, but there was some experimental stuff which may or may not work. She helped him pack as he talked. He mentioned unfamiliar terms: AZT, drug trials, T-cells, viral load. He didn't know when or where he had contracted it, probably right before entering the Peace Corps. Realizing that she desperately wanted to help him through this, she calculated that she would return home in another nine months.

"Where will you be?" She asked him.

"My family is near Boston, and I can get good care there."

"Okay," she said. "I'll see you there in nine months."

"Rosie, you don't have to—"

"I couldn't have made it a year here without you. I think I owe you."

He looked relieved. Not all the volunteers would be as accepting of his diagnosis. She wouldn't tell anyone, just as she had kept silent about his sexual preferences, and he thanked her. "So I guess I'll see you there," she said.

"In Boston?"

"Boston."

She arrives at the top of the hill they've been climbing and is aware of how hard she's breathing. Meanwhile, Art has made himself comfortable on a boulder and has obviously not even begun to sweat. Together they admire the scene before them. The jagged Maine coastline is below. There are scattered islands and beyond these stretches of rock and tree all the way to the Atlantic Ocean. Closer to where they sit, the breeze moves the trees, and some of the tops begin to look bare. The air is still warm, though, and she sits beside Art on the granite summit.

"I just wish . . ." she begins, but doesn't know how to finish. Art looks down, picks up a pebble, and tosses it over the side. They watch it disappear.

"What?" he asks, finally.

"Just, I don't know, that I weren't so helpless."

"I don't think you're the first to feel that way when someone dies of a disease at an early age."

"But I mean, there were times when I wanted to know more, to explain to him. To help him toward the end, when he couldn't think right." Her thoughts are disjointed. "I want to do more."

"Like what?"

"Like, interpret those crazy tests for them. And like, when Octavius got information of drug trials, I wish I could have known which would work."

"Don't the doctors know that?"

"Yeah, I guess."

"Didn't they do that?"

"Not in a way that made it more understandable, or more obvious what we should do, anyway. They talked science and statistics, which made it sound more complicated."

"You figured it out, though, right?"

"Not enough. And not so I could be, I don't know, fighting the fight." The mountain is quiet. He releases another pebble which dances down the granite, a sound halfway between a crack and a bounce. "That expression doesn't work for me," he states finally.

"Which one?"

"'Fighting the fight.' You're not talking about an event with a beginning and an end. And it makes it sound like it's a soap opera or something."

"But everyone talks about 'the battle against AIDS.' It's not like I made it up."

"No. But do you really think it was a battle for Octavius? I didn't see him at the end like you did; it sounds more like he withered."

"He did. And I wish I could have done more."

"So there you go. You have a degree in science. Go to medical school." Rosie opens her mouth, then closes it. She looks at him. "Rosie, you've been talking like this for awhile. You second-guessed everything, from the beginning, and you talked about, well, basically, wanting to be in charge. So be in charge." He looks at her and she meets the challenge in his eyes. But she blinks and looks away, "But what if . . ."

He interrupts her, "But what if you end up on top of a mountain again, asking the same question, and just wishing."

Rosie rubs the tears from the corner of her eyes, sniffles, and nods. "Medical school. All right." She sits straighter. "All right."

It's three days later and she's in the apartment, stirring Ramen noodles into a pot and listening to music. Returning to work on Monday had been a relief. She had a temporary position processing samples in a lab for a research project. The hum of the equipment and the methodical work soothed her, and made her thoughts clearer and memories less jagged, less threatening. The work is often tedious and boring. Every now and then, though, she appreciates what it provides: essentially, mental sanctity. Her co-workers in the lab provide just enough interpersonal interaction, and they retreat to their stations after brief conversations or excursions for lunch or coffee.

The door opens and she hears her roommate toss her keys on the table. Anna walks into the living room, her scrubs wrinkled and her hair frizzing out of her ponytail.

"How was your day?" Rosie asks from the adjoining kitchen.

"My feet hurt." She collapses onto the sofa. Rosie walks in with her bowl of noodles. "Gourmet again?" Anna asks her.

"Uh hunh." She sits on the floor near the end of the coffee table, crosses her legs, and puts her bowl in front of her. "Want some?"

"No thanks." Anna tosses off her shoes and rubs her toes.

"You're home late," Rosie observes. "Work overtime again?"

"Yeah, Cathy had a crisis with her kids again, so I covered for her until she got there."

"Did you have a good weekend at least?"

"Oh, it was great. Nice to get away, especially when everyone else is working." Since Anna works weekends, she takes Monday and Tuesday off, and they both refer to it as the weekend in the traditional sense.

"So what were you going to tell me? Some epiphany on top of a mountain?" She leans back on the pillows, crosses her arms, and looks expectantly at Rosie.

"I'm thinking about medical school."

"Medical school?" Anna's eyebrows rise. "Why is God's name would you want to do that?"

Rosie explains the conversation she had had with Art, and how it had led to the conclusion of going to medical school. She had spent the last three days fantasizing about walking down hospital hallways, her white coat flying like a cape behind her. She imagined her confidence and satisfaction as she saved lives. But as she talks to Anna, the excitement and enthusiasm fizzles. The idea begins to seem silly, even ridiculous. The career choice had brought hope and a sense of peace to her, and the disappointment as it loses its power is deep and heavy. "You think it's a dumb idea?" she asks.

"No, not dumb. Just, doctors aren't always all they're cracked up to be. Some are fantastic, yes, but you should meet some of the students we have to work with. It's like, they don't know what else to do, and they want to make money and stay elite, so they go to medical school. You should have seen this chick the other day. She drops her coffee on the floor, and looks at me, and says, 'well aren't you going to clean that up?'"

"Harvard?" Anna's look answers the question.

"And, it's a while before you're practicing on your own. Then there's the debt . . ." Rosie's disappointment grows and she stares into her soup, embarrassed by the tears that begin to form.

"Look," says Anna, leaning forward. She pulls her hair from her ponytail and rakes her fingers through her hair for a few moments, then sighs. "It's like, health care is this huge beast, and you have to look at it from all the angles. Most people automatically think 'doctor' when they think of the people on the front lines of patient care: the ones calling the shots. But there are other ways to do patient care, especially the kind you're taking about."

Rosie looks up, still trying to hide her disappointment, and begins to feel a new hope as Anna continues to explain the many facets of health care and providing patient care.

"You want to do hands on care, right?"

Rosie nods. "I want to be able to take care of someone like Octavius. That's sort of what sparked this whole thing."

"Okay. AIDS work. And you thought about being a case worker or a patient advocate?"

"Well, no, not really. I'm interested in more than advocacy. I don't want to feel like my hands are tied, again, ever."

"How do you mean?"

"I mean if a patient needs a medicine, I don't want to have to beg and plead with the doctor to prescribe it. I'd want that authority."

"Hmm," Anna leans back again. "There's a nurse on my floor—Regina--who's in graduate school to become a nurse practitioner."

"Nurse practitioner?" Rosie asks. She thinks of the person in scrubs who came in to take Octavius' blood pressure every four hours. "I thought that was like, an assistant to a nurse or something."

Anna shakes her head. "Actually, it's more than what a nurse does. Nurse practitioners do almost what the doctor does. Except bring home the pay check." Anna winks at her and she laughs.

"So I have to go to nursing school?" She'd seen plenty of what the nurses did, and, although she admired it, she didn't really want this role.

"Not necessarily. Where Regina is going, there's a program specifically for people with degrees in something other than nursing. They go for three years and get both an RN and NP education."

"Hmm." Rosie looks thoughtful and eats her soup.

"The thing is, Rose, you know exactly what you want to do. Nurse practitioners make good money, have less debt, and can work pretty independently, but they still have supervision when they need it. If you go to medical school . . .. It's just a long haul, and at some point you're going to find yourself doing something like putting in a central line, and you'll feel like you're wasting your time."

Rosie thinks about how Octavius' greatest pet peeve was people who waste their time in life. He had said it was a human being's greatest waste of resources. A mind not used and a talent purposely hidden, he'd said, were like litter on a beach: unnecessary and irritating to see. She calculates that, since she is 29 now, she could be out practicing as a nurse practitioner at age 32. If she chooses medical school, she won't be practicing on her own for at least eight years. Somehow 37 seems so much older. The CD she has been listening to ends and the apartment is unusually quiet. Rosie jumps when Anna turns on the TV with the remote.

"Why don't you talk to her." Anna says, looking at the screen.

"Who?" Rosie has difficulty leaving her thoughts and re-entering the conversation.

"Regina. I'm sure she'll be happy to tell you about the program."

"Okay." She straightens her legs and leans back on her hands.

It's a hard decision and she agonizes over it. Talking to Regina at length makes her excited about the graduate program. That enthusiasm ebbs when, at work, she attends a research meeting and is impressed by the physicians and the respect they command. After the meeting, she talks to one of the doctors who leads the research project. He is a scientist, regularly wearing a bowtie and jacket, and the conversation is unnatural and awkward. At grand rounds at the adjacent hospital, she finds the resident's presentation uninspiring. Her appreciation of the research doesn't match her drive to do direct patient care, even though she can picture herself in the same white coat, voicing over slides in a dimly lit room and reviewing data. Walking along the Charles one Saturday afternoon in early November, she gazes at the blue water and the sailboats braving the cold and wonders if she'd have time to enjoy such an afternoon as a medical student. And then there's the next morning—Sunday--when she rolls out of bed at 9:00am, strolls to the neighborhood coffee shop, and leisurely reads the Boston Globe. She cherishes her sleep and the lazy mornings that occasionally follow it.

She puts down the front page, holds her latte, and stares toward the floor. The door opens and a couple walks in, holding hands. They stand close to one another by the counter and the woman wraps her arm through his as they ponder the menu board. They're dressed for the colder day with hats and long, warm coats with gloves. Rosie is aware of the empty chair at her table, and feels her loneliness. For three years, she's been unavailable, her heart focused on a gay man dying of AIDS. It's odd to have weekends alone, even though she had wanted time off. She'd spent so many Saturdays and Sundays going to and from the hospital to see him. Watching this couple, she wonders how her career decision may continue to make her unavailable. Would medical school leave enough time to date? The idea of dating a fellow student seems incestuous. As she thinks of her upcoming 30th birthday, her single status brings anxiety and a beginning desperation. The couple looks young and athletic, and this observation makes Rosie feel worn out and dull. She sighs with such expression that she then quickly looks around to make sure no one has noticed.

When she leaves the shop, the wind has picked up and the cold moves straight through her as she quickly walks home. The sun had been out earlier, but now there are clouds. Brown leaves swirl noisily in clusters by the base of naked trees. A cold front is moving in. She's had the thought recently that she can leave this cold and lonely city. Even in the hot days of summer, it doesn't feel warm. She glances at the formal architecture, which makes her even more uneasy and out of place. New beginnings excite her. Whatever she does next, she's confident it won't be in Boston.

On a Friday night, she and Anna go out. They meet at Billy Ray's, where there's live jazz and an eclectic mix of college students, young professionals, and black people from the neighborhood which abuts it. Rosie arrives early, since she's done with work and ready to go out. The crowd has yet to arrive, since it's only 6:00 o'clock and the band won't start until 9:00. At about 8:30, there will be a line out the door and to the end of the block of people waiting to get in. She sits down at the bar next to a black man in a long coat, who wears a black Fedora partially covering his short graying hair. He has glasses, and they look like bifocals, she thinks, when he turns to talk to her. They exchange first names and talk about the bar, the neighborhood, and the kinds of bands which play there. He tells her he used to play the guitar. His fingers are thick, and bent with arthritis. They talk about the cold winters, and he says how his joints hurt from October to May. She smiles sympathetically and shakes her head at this discomfort. He's from Louisiana, he tells her, and thinking of going back, but then, he says, no place is perfect. As strangers they enjoy a conversation with no pressure to continue, and there are long silences during which they sit without talking, occasionally sipping on their drinks. It's almost the end of happy hour, and the bar is starting to fill. He buys her a drink, but since she's not done with the one she has, the bartender overturns a shot glass where she's sitting. He pays his bill, shakes her hand and says, "Nice talking to you, Miss Rosie." She echoes this intention with sincerity.

No place is perfect, she thinks, as he leaves. She realizes this concept is true of many things. No place, no person, and no decision. She is aware that with his first mention of arthritis, she wanted somehow to help him and improve his quality of life. She is thankful for the time to enjoy a leisurely conversation with a stranger. It's very clear to her, suddenly, in that moment, that she wants to become a nurse practitioner. She wants to spend time with patients, she wants to improve on the quality of their lives, and she wants to cure with nurturing as much as with science. She turns the shot glass over and the bartender soon reaches for it. "Another Lagga?" he asks, and she nods with a slight smile. He pours another Sam Adams for her and she watches it run from the tap. The bartender has begun to move faster, and he looks toward the end of the bar as he pours, not at her, as he hurriedly leaves the drink in front of her. For the first time in more than a month, she completely relaxes, sinking into the moment, finally confident with resolution. She looks in the mirror behind the bar, peering between bottles of whisky and vodka that double themselves in the reflection. Anna's image appears backwards as she steps through the door. People are drifting in like a tide, approaching the bar, leaning in to get the bartender's attention. Just before Rosie turns to greet her friend, she looks into her reflection and silently and imperceptibly toasts her decision.

She's dreaming of a river. The water rushes by, thundering over rocks and branches. The color of the stones blurs in the current. Then she hears her name. Someone is calling her and she recognizes the voice. Looking all around, she finally sees him, moving his arms above his head, smiling from the other side of the river. It's Octavius, young and healthy—younger, even, than when they met, and he's waving and shouting to her. She looks down and starts to step across. It's only about twenty feet, but the current is fast. "Jump!" he cups his mouth with his hands and yells, and she looks at him then down at her feet. How can she jump that far? The water's movement makes her dizzy. She looks up again and the distance has doubled—no, tripled. There's no way she can make it across, and she's terrified since she's farther away from the bank. He's there on the opposite bank, then he's not—there are too many trees and shrubs and she can't hear him. Her voice is lost in the sound of the water as she struggles to yell for him. She extends her arms as she loses her balance and twists to right herself. Where is he? And then he's there in front of her, extending a hand, leading her across the torrents. Stepping and showing her where to step, he turns to wink at her the way he always did. The rush of the river becomes a song and his smile is the sun. In the next moment they are on the other side. The river slows to a lullaby. Light surrounds them now. "Well," he says. "Come on."

2.

October, 1998

Rosie rides her bike down to Ocean Beach just after the sun comes up. Her 21-speed road bike has been her smartest purchase since starting graduate school two months ago. The black gloves are already well worn, and they smell of leather and sweat. She takes them off, along with her grey helmet when she arrives at the parking area. There are only a few cars here, and she can see some people with fishing poles along the beach. It's too early to be windy or foggy, and she admires the colors of the early morning sky for a moment before locking her bicycle to a nearly post. She will make this early morning ride and meditative walk on the anniversary of his death a ceremonious ritual each year. Changing out of her clip cycling shoes, she slips on the Tevas that she's carried in her backpack. Slowly, she'll walk the path along the bluff, thinking of Octavius, and then follow a path down to the ocean.

The Pacific is different from the Atlantic, she thinks as she walks, yet somehow very similar. The cliffs are higher here, and the panoramic view from the bluff always enthralls her, more so than the Atlantic. The day is just beginning; when she mounted her bike this morning only street lights illuminated the day. She starts up the path, where there's succulent ground cover and crooked trees growing at odd angles where they're exposed to the wind. The paved path has sandy areas, and the white sand is fine and gritty under her feet, sticking to her skin when she inadvertently kicks it up. When she gets to the top of the path, she turns and walks back, and, when she is almost back to where she started, she finds the sandy path to the left that descends dramatically to the beach. The waves crash on sand here, but north and south there are areas of worn and jagged rock where the water swirls, turns, and froths. The Pacific intimidates her, just like the cold Atlantic waters with ripping currents in northern Maine. The magnificent force both humbles and assures her. In a low, thick voice it seems to say: "You're not that powerful."

Today she walks to the water and to squat down and touch the edge of the wave that climbs up the sand. Its cool, frothy feel is like touching the fingers of the universe. Although his ashes were scattered more than 3,000 miles away, she feels that he is here, and that she is part of the changes that occur through all of time. The roar of the ocean soothes her, and the monotony brings her thoughts to a pause. She closes her eyes, and gives thanks that she could know him. How he changed my life, she thinks, and smiles while she blinks back tears. The moment is long and holy, and then it is gone. The pressures of the day assault her.

36

She has class in two hours. After that, her volunteer work begins. Turning once to look at the ocean before resigning herself to the day, she walks back up the path. She reaches her bicycle, changes her shoes, dons her gloves and helmet, and pedals back home.

A shower, clean clothes, deodorant, notebook, water bottle, apple, twisting her hair together to clump it in a hairclip at the back of her head. The keys jingle for the moments between the table and the pocket of her jeans. She gets back on her bike, and rides the up and down three quarters of a mile to school. Nursing assessment has been exciting since the first day, when she and her thirty-one classmates sat anxiously with books and paper, tossing around weak smiles to unfamiliar faces. It had reminded her of that first Peace Corps meeting, but now the group was mostly comprised of women and eccentric personalities were difficult to spot. The instructor had strolled in, followed by four clinical instructors, in white lab coats, each with their clipboard of names and obviously comfortable and at ease with each other. There had been an audible coming to attention of the class as the five arranged themselves in the front of the room.

Roll call had been followed by an acknowledgment of their hopes and fears in the class as well as in the career of a nurse practitioner.

"Some of you have chosen to enroll because of the promise of a lucrative career, while others have been drawn to it because of an innate or maybe even urgent need to provide care for patients," Ms. Sharrico had stated. Rosie involuntary nodded. "But in our experience," she looked at the clinical instructors, who nodded their heads almost simultaneously as she said, "the first obstacles that students want to overcome are, procedures. Blood draws, dressing changes, injections, all of that hands on stuff that makes you shake and sweat." Laughter meekly arose from the chairs, followed by a number of voiced consents and head bobbing. "So, without further ado," a conspicuous look passed from instructor to instructor as they fanned out across the front of the class, reached into to pockets of their lab coats, and began to distribute syringes with short, fine needles, bottles of saline, and alcohol pads. The syringes were wrapped in plastic with a paper backing describing the contents. "First, never, ever, under any circumstances WHATSOEVER . . ." the mutterings stopped and all eyes faced forward, "NEVER recap a needle."

They had proceeded to learn how to draw air into the needle first, then wipe the top of the saline bottle, puncture it, invert it, push out the air and carefully withdraw the same amount of fluid. They had sat tap tapping out air bubbles on the edge of frustration, leading to laughter and the release of tension. Lastly, they had divided into groups and followed instructors to the lab, where they partnered up, and with sweaty hands resisting latex gloves, wiped the backs of their partners upper arms with alcohol pads, pinched a springy layer of flesh, and inserted the needles at 45 degrees and pushed in the fluid. Rosie followed the needle carefully with her eyes once she withdrew it, as instructed, and deposited in the sharps container. Bandaids followed, and they returned to class relieved, excited, and then amused to find miniature lollipops at their desks.

The moments of giving her first injection were vivid, with emotions like a near miss car crash. She'd had sweaty palms and a racing heart that gradually balanced back to normal when she'd grasped that everything was going to be okay. Drawing the saline into the syringe had been easy, and almost meditative in the effortless concentration. But her hand trembled in the lab as she wiped her partner's arm, a friendly-faced blond woman who nervously uttered words of encouragement. She had felt that, somehow, she needed a third arm as she located and used the alcohol pad, then the syringe, and finally the cotton ball. The needle shook as she inserted it as quickly as she could, then pushed in the saline and hoped the woman couldn't feel her unintentional movement. The fact that she received the same assault from her partner made the task easier, and absolved her guilt of pain inflicted. When she placed the cotton ball over the tiny wound, her hands held still in the now slimy gloves but she could feel her heart still pound. Despite all of her anxiety and trepidation, the rush of relief, the "I can DO this!" sensation seared through her like a drug.

Back in the classroom, the instructor leaned on an unoccupied desk at the front of the class, waiting for the last few individuals to return. The crinkling paper sound filled the air as students stuck the suckers in their mouths. Without saying anything, Ms. Sharrico commanded attention. She had an intensity and strength like water. When the room was quiet, she looked around at her students, many now slouching, some with an expectant smile, pens poised, and none of the pen tapping or leg bouncing that the class had begun with. Already, there was cohesion that would last the two years of their schooling and beyond. "Better?" She asked. Nods, "yeah's", and one mock hysterical "my arm hurts!!!" followed by an exaggerated shove and giggles. "Alright, then." Ms. Sharrico stood and walked behind the podium. "Nursing assessment . . .".

Now Rosie locks her bike outside of the building and walks in to class. Today's lecture topic is the respiratory system. They've been through initial assessment of the patient; learning to look at the patient immediately and ignore the beeps, buzzes, and sucks of machines as they determined basic elements of health and well-being. Taking vital signs had followed, then cardiac exam, with pulses all over the body in places

Rosie hadn't realized the beating heart could be felt. Today in class, as Ms. Sharrico had demostrated with heart sounds, the lights are dimmed and an audio tract of respiratory sounds plays. The voice over meditatively announces what they hear: rales, rhonchi, egophony, wheezes. She plays the tract three times as if initiating them into a cult of abnormal breathing. The lecture ensues, with discussion of pneumonia, asthma, lung cancer, pneumothorax, chest tubes, and empyema along with appropriate care of patients with these ailments. The students write vigorously in their notebooks, and hands rise to discuss clinical scenarios students have encountered in their clinical assignments on the hospital floor. When the class is over, they move to the lab, where, again, they meet with partners to don stethoscopes and enter the quiet wholeness of another being's breath. Listening to breathing mimics listening to the ocean waves on a calm day. The in and out of breath mesmerizes like the crash and pull of water. Heart sounds accompany breath like sea gulls calls, only with steady rhythm. The gentle lullaby quality of these sounds assures them that, just as Ms. Sharrico promises, diagnoses will jump out at them, provided they listen. Rosie listens, washed with calm and the delicious sensation that where she stands, next to the exam table with her stethoscope on the back of her partner, and what she does now, training to be a nurse practitioner, is absolutely perfect for her.

There are the clinical assignments, referred to as "clinicals." Once a week, they put on their green or blue scrubs and supportive shoes and arrive anxious, bleary-eyed, and nauseous because it's the end of the week and they're sleepless and unaccustomed to the pervasive hospital smell. They gather against the wall and dusty windowsill of the conference room, to listen with the nurses to report. The overhead fluorescent light contrasts with the sunrise outside the window. Books and journals lay scattered around the room, and there's a sink and refrigerator in the corner. One nurse sits by the tape player, clicking it on and off to repeat the voice of the nurse describing the needs or condition of the patient she has now left when her shift ended. The tape gets flicked off when a question is asked. The students don't ask questions. One thing they have learned is that, other than their clinical instructor, nurses don't particularly like fledgling nurses. Early in class, the hear the phrase, "nurses eat their young." They strike whenever the opportunity arises to point out weaknesses, flaws, or what they think is stupidity. The registered nurses on the floor harbor tight, intimate relationships with each other but seem to view the students as temporary inconveniences who, if ignored, will eventually go away.

On the morning of her first clinical she's early. The clock in the entrance shows 6:30 when she walks through the revolving door, so she turns right toward the coffee shop instead of left to the elevators. Rosie stands behind a tall, muscular man in green scrubs with a stethoscope around his neck, and she's halfway to deciding that he's a doctor and maybe surgeon when he turns enough for her to recognize him. "Richard?" she asks. Her classmate turns to face her and smile. "Hey!" he says, and they begin a discussion on how the sun isn't quite up so they shouldn't be and how they hope they don't ruin their first day at clinical by spilling coffee down their shirt.

At the front of the line, Richard addresses the barrister by name. He nods an assent when the man asks him if he wants his usual. Rosie gets her coffee and they head off to the elevators.

"You must have been here before," Rosie says.

"Yeah. Too many times!" he takes a sip of his drink, a vanilla latte. "And not always good times."

"I'm sorry."

He looks up at the lights above the elevator. She's not sure how to communicate empathy without prying. The elevator arrives and they ride to their floor in silence. Richard is sarcastic and jovial, she learns, and he breaks the silence and eases them back to their previous banter.

The way the nurses form an impervious click encourages the students to do the same. When they have their own group meeting in the conference room, the intimate details of their lives are shared. Within the first month of their assignment, Richard reveals to the group of seven that he's been on this medical/surgical floor previously, when his partner was ill. He talks of Paul as if he's a friend to all of them. The loss is still new; Richard brought his love home just over a year ago so he could die with hospice care at home.

"He forgot everything," Richard tells them. "How to talk, how to stand up, how to sit down. Getting him in and out of a car was a nightmare. I had to have two nurses and a PT help me when we left the doctor's office. Then he got awful fevers on top of the PML—"

"What's PML?" one of the other students asks.

"Progressive multifactorial leukoencephalopathy," Rosie answers automatically, staring at the off-white table. Richard looks at her with shock and an odd significant hope. They bond in the moment that she meets his eyes and explains, "My friend died with that, too." He nods. Someone slurps coffee. A tissue is pulled out of its box. "Octavius." The tears start again as she shares the memory.

She can't tell if the smell is there or if it's something she imagines. The elevator is hushed; five strangers, two in blue scrubs that hang off their shoulders and drag to the ground, face the metal doors. The elevator moves up and they look to the numbers that flash above the door seemingly without thought. The numbers 6, 7, and 14 are lit up in red beside the door. Movement stops as "6" appears in white above the door. They rattle open with a groan to reveal white tile and the noises of the floor. "Excuse me," Rosie says, and shoulders her way through the people who part to let her pass.

The doors close and the smell hits her. The one so intense she feels it in her sleep. It's viscerally memorable, like the smell of diesel in Africa, rising from engines in thick, black puffs that clung to her skin and the inside of her nostrils. Anytime she smells it now she's sent reeling back in time for various durations of moments. Now, she breathes in the hospital smell, a combination of things wickedly clean and horridly dirty. The hand soap, the laundry soap, disinfectant, adhesive, and a scent like the depths of human bowels cling together in the air she breathes. It drowns out even feces in its stench. It's like the smell of a body turned inside out. It takes the human nose three minutes to numb to any fragrance, and for three minutes there's a pause before each inhalation she takes, as her nervous system reluctantly allows her to breathe. She steps around the yellow inverted "V" sign with a red figure warning her of slippery floors and she turns at the nurses station.

Room 632. The door is partly open and the lights are off. He doesn't make sense anymore. The frail, semi-conscious man in the bed is barely recognizable. She touches his pale hand on the bed and feels self conscious as she says, "Octavius, it's me, Rosie." There's a mumbling from his lips but nothing else. His lips are white with think saliva and dried skin and she takes the swab next to his bed and runs it over his mouth carefully, softly, like a kiss. She pulls out a book of poetry. Not knowing what else to do, she spends her visits reading to him, wracking her brain to remember writers he's mentioned or quoted. Today she has T.S. Eliot. The more she reads, the less self-conscious she feels. But in the middle of her reading he turns to her, slowly, and says in a tired and slurring voice, "they're coming, you know."

She looks toward the door, thinking he means a gurney to carry him away for another test. "Who?"

He looks past her, out the window at the blue sky and white clouds and bright, bright light. "The angels."

Tears form and she forces herself not to turn around and look, but to face him. "What do you mean?" she half-smiles at him.

"They're coming for me." It's slurred and whispered, but she doesn't dare ask him to repeat himself. The hair on her arms is standing up and the back of her neck is exquisitely sensitive, so much so that she imagines a breeze in the still, tired air of the hospital floor. She wants to say something reassuring or wise but can't think of a thing. He's not looking at her but she feels she can't gaze at him. She looks at the book, rubs her nose with the heel of her palm, then looks at him. The I.V. fluids drip in smoothly, reassuringly. Unable to resist, she glances over her shoulder and sees only the sky. She's lost her place in the poem. Several minutes pass. Footsteps in the hall, a TV from the next room, voices from the nurse's station, and she imagines she hears his every breath. She turns the pages, looks at him, and, not knowing what else to do, begins to read again: "Let us go then, you and I , as the evening spread itself against the sky--"

"It's cold in here." He murmurs.

"I'll, um, I'll find you a blanket." She puts the book down, scanning the room with her eyes. Boxes of latex gloves, the alcohol hand sanitizer dispense, the dark TV that looks like an eye socket hovering above them. She moves around the room, looking.

"Cold." He says. Where are they? She's seen a nurse get one before. She peeks into the bathroom. Nothing. Finally, she looks up and there they are, neatly folded sterile humps of white. Her hand pulls at air when she turns dramatically to him as he says:

"Too cold for the weather."

Rosie and her classmates trudge to and from class and clinicals, taking exams, writing papers, visibly growing weary from the intensity of this learning. Rosie obtains a part time position entering data for the research department, and for ten hours a week she sits in front of the computer in a small office with a stack of labs and tries hard not to confuse the numbers with the values. She blinks hard every thirty seconds and takes breaks every fifteen sheets. She takes a blank, white sheet of paper to line up the numbers. It's dull and methodical, in addition to challenging with her sleep deprived state, but anything more demanding would overthrow a balance that she's barely achieved. On rare clear days, when she can, she rides her bike over the Golden Gate Bridge, then turns left to climb the hill and gaze back at the city and the blue bay. It gives her perspective and helps her remain calm through exams and clinical procedures. Riding down, rhythmically squeezing the brake levers, the moving air gives her freedom. She sings to herself as she floats down the switch backed hill.

They rotate through clinicals. In the spring, they are in the pediatric unit with sick kids who are often bored or want nothing but to play. The parents are despondent. Rosie's decision to take care of only adults is confirmed as her heart breaks for the small bodies curled in the beds with IV lines attached to their limbs, red-eyed mothers and fathers by their sides. In class, they discuss illness in children, and the instructor is supportive and patient. The stories the professor shares of her own experiences bring tears, laughter, and incredulousness. The personal touch makes the two-hour class bearable and the exams easier.

The program Rosie takes is accelerated, and they attend class and rotate through clinicals during the summer. In labor and delivery, the smells, sounds, and flurry of different bodies in scrubs moving in and out of the room makes Rosie think that she'll give birth at a birthing center if the moment ever comes. She enters a room with a nurse and the young woman is in the throws of the final stages of labor, being coached by a nurse midwife and the woman's aunt. The boyfriend is nervously hanging back by the head of the bed, waiting for instructions, which he promptly follows, practically landing on the bed as he trips over his feet in the process. At the end of a contraction, the nurse midwife explains the she has to go, because her shift is over, and she introduces the obstetrician who will take over. The woman barely nods, breathes, and begins to contract again. The obstetrician enters with a resident and medical student in tow, and as Rosie thinks, "it's getting kind of crowded" the pediatrician wheels in with a cart and her own resident and medical student. Moments later, the baby boy is born, pink and healthy and sucking in air to surprise himself with a very healthy cry. Rosie's focus is on the mom, who collapses with exhaustion and closes her eyes.

It's a long year for Rosie, and when September comes it feels as though she's known her classmates longer than twelve months. They collect at each other's apartments to study for the nurse's licensing exam, the NCLEX, which will officially make them registered nurses. They pour over pre-exam sample tests, discuss topics, drink coffee, make popcorn, order pizza, and open wine at the end of it all when their brain's are too saturated with information to do anything more. They tell jokes and share stories, noting how they can talk about ugly dressing changes they've done in clinical, involving puss and blood, and continue eating pepperoni pizza.

They get a week off from class and clinical in September during which they're encouraged to sit for their NCLEX exam. Rosie and her roommates go together, and they're lead to a small, carpeted room with cubby-hole computer stations. A friendly attendant smiles warmly when they enter, encourages them to relax, and offers them pencils and paper to take notes. She points the direction to the bathroom, and leads them each to a computer station. There's one person in the room already who they don't recognize, and they enter quietly.

Rosie sits down at the computer. She feels cold and shaky. She's so afraid she'll fail. Her eyes feel dry, her stomach feels upside down, and she thinks maybe she should have gone to the restroom a third time.

"Ready?" she's asked. "I think so." The attendant taps some keys, clicks on some icons, and the exam pops up. Rosie begins.

The questions pop up, one after another. Some are easy, some she re-reads four or five times to try to determine what they're asking. The answers are sometimes obvious, and at other times, "near" answers. Should she wash her hands for 15 or 25 seconds? The instructors warned them about these types of questions, where the correct answer would be missing and they would need to pick a close second. Then there are the questions that frighten her and make her sweat because she simply does not know how to answer them, and the multiple choices make the questions more convoluted. She encounters more of these as she continues, making her angry, anxious, and bringing to mind visions of herself heading east, when she fails and needs to hang her head and travel home. I should really buy a used car, she thinks. She blinks away the vision, shakes her head, and carries on. In two hours it is over.

The exam is structured so that there are a grand total of questions, but if a person answers enough of a percentage correctly after a certain number, the test shuts off. Of course, the opposite is also true; if enough of a percentage is wrong you would also be told you were finished. She and her roommates leave feeling worse than when they had arrived.

In class, the mood is grim. There are a few students who have chosen to wait to take the exam, and the reports from those who have taken it discourage them from taking it any time soon. The memory distracts Rosie, and she finds herself losing focus in class and daydreaming. She thinks of Florida, where her parents are, and imagines lying on the beach or maybe finally learning to surf.

Two weeks later, there it is, in the mail. Three envelopes, one for each of them, the return address from the American Nursing Association. She tears open her envelope and anxiously scans it, beginning to smile as she realizes there's a card enclosed. A thin plastic card reads "Domenica Rose Petroni, RN. She begins to breathe again.

October, 1999

By the beginning of the last year of her graduate school, a new era has donned in HIV and AIDS, and she's constantly reminded of how Octavius just missed these new drugs that are extending patient's lives, perhaps to a normal lifespan. They have to take several pills a day, often three times a day, but they are alive and thriving. Genotyping and phenotyping are available now, enabling clinicians to determine which key medicines a patient with HIV should receive.

She arrives at class and pulls out her assignment. Today is another anniversary, and she's already weary from her journey to the ocean and the memories that now have more meaning given her newfound clinical understanding of illness. She slumps down next to Richard.

"Hi Honey!" he says, patting her arm. Although the classes and clinical assignments have created many strong friendships, she only shared this anniversary day with him. Telling others reduces its meaning, and she doesn't want it to lose that importance.

"Hey, Richard," she smiles, grateful for his friendship. He had offered to meet her at the beach, and she had declined.

"How was your morning?" His sincerity is heartwarming.

"Okay," she says, then corrects her self. "Actually, it was really nice. Peaceful, in fact." She leans back in her seat and sighs. "That's kind of surprising, hunh?"

"No, I don't think so. When Paul died, I thought I'd never feel happiness again. But it happened, even at moments when I missed him the most." He shakes his head at this irony. "Just like his death, a lot of it doesn't make sense. Anyway," he reaches into his backpack and pulls out a paper pastry bag to hand to her, "this is for you."

She opens it and pulls out a chocolate chip bagel and laughs. It's touching that he would take care of her this way. She leans toward him and hugs him. "Thanks."

The instructor walks in and the chatter tapers off as eyes turn toward the end of the table. This class, The Face of HIV: Psychosocial Aspects of HIV, is a fairly small, intimate group. Ten classmates sit around an oval conference table. There are no windows, and when the door shuts, the closeness they feel deepens. If no one talks, there is absolute silence, and the privacy is reassuring.

"Good morning," the instructor begins, sitting down and looking around the table. "How is everyone today?" There are smiles and nods and a few answers of "good." "Let's start with the what's new in HIV presentation." She looks down at an assignment book. "Rosie? You ready?"

Rosie nods, clears her throat, and briefly outlines a new drug for HIV that is in experimental stages. It will reduce pill burden for patients, so they will only have to take this drug twice a day, with three pills each time. They'll have to take two other drugs as well, but at most this will amount to an additional two pills with each dose. Five pills, twice a day, is an improvement in this class of drug. Even more impressive is that this new medicine will work where its competitors have failed. This improvement means more saved lives. Rosie reviews the side effects, which are slightly discouraging, but not a surprise, and actually minimal when measured against its competitors.

There are nods and smiles around the room, with one student mumbling, it's about time. Everyone laughs at this remark, then they look at the instructor expectantly. "Thanks, Rosie," she says. "So, how will this change our field? How will our patients react to this news?" There are responses around the room, one-word utterances such as "hope," "relief," and "courage." This is the class that runs on its own energy, and the hour and a half go by unnoticed. The dialogue prepares them to address their patient's emotional responses to HIV infection. It will help them teach coping skills, and personal acceptance of what the diagnosis means. They discuss how the disease affects their society and their patient's psyche, in addition to their own.

"There's a patient in my clinic on that." Heads turn to listen to Linda, a woman with long, straight, brown hair who is a year behind Rosie in the program. Linda has a calm demeanor, and her patients always like her. "He's having a hard time, though, because he's getting better."

"What do you mean?" asks Richard. "Like, feeling guilty?"

"Yeah," she says, nodding her head. "Extremely so. He has this long list of friends who are dead and he doesn't know why he's still here."

The instructor stands and writes on the board "Lazarus Syndrome." She describes this phenomenon as a common conflict people with HIV face. They are grateful for their care, but they feel guilty that they've survived. It's a "why me?" question that leans toward existentialism.

"I'd like to help him, though, since he seems so depressed by it. What do I say to him?" Linda asks, and her face shows her genuine concern.

It's a tough question, and they talk about possible answers. They conclude that the answer is extremely personal, and not any different from the question that has been asked for decades; why are we here? Is not new to the human race.

"The important thing to do," the instructor states as the class draws to a close, "is to be present with him. Offer to listen, and communicate that concern that you feel. Pay attention to what he says, and validate his emotions. This will go a long way in helping him to heal.

"Not long ago, maybe three years ago, I used to bring a box of tissues to this class. We spent the whole time talking about who had died. Now we talk about who's alive, which is a different kind of challenge. But the thing that's the same is that we're still talking about healing, and what that means. Linda, if your patient can answer that question for himself, he's done a lot of healing. If you can help him get there, you're doing a lot to provide complete care.

"Alright, time's up." She looks down at her assignment book to determine who is next to present to the class. Rosie hands in her drug review, and there are sounds of chairs moving as people get up to leave. "Everyone have a good week." The instructor smiles, closing her book.

Dr. Davids is already loading the van when she arrives at the clinic. She takes the Muni, since they will return after dark. She hurries to help him carry boxes of latex gloves, blood vials, and samples of a pink packaged pill called azithromycin to the van. It's a large vehicle without rear seats and resembles an ambulance, which allows them to see patients in the back. There isn't enough headroom to stand, but they can sit or

have a patient lie down on a cot. She has a clinical assignment with Dr.

Davids, who runs a public health clinic for homeless people, many with

HIV. He is well known throughout the community, and she has so much

respect for him that she has difficulty starting or continuing a

conversation with him. In general, he doesn't talk much, but he forms

close relationships with his patients and commits as much time as he can

to his clinic. His stoicism enhances the power of his words; when he tells

stories of patients he's seen and known, she and other students listen

intently. He's an older doctor, close to retiring, with a scruffy salt and

pepper beard and mustache that usually hangs over his upper lip. His hair

is thinning, and he regularly brushes his hand over his head as if to check

how much is still there. His disheveled office, where she has a clinical

assignment one day a week, is crowded with books and journals. Above

his desk hangs pictures of him with his three children, when they, and he,

were younger. The pictures are full of smiles, and most show a toddler or

young child hanging around his neck in an embrace. He speaks of them

fondly.

This evening they will head over to the park, first. They keep a

fairly regular schedule, so that if a person needs them, they can be found.

She sees the patients with him, learning how to hear abnormal sounds in

their lungs, to listen for heart murmurs, and to detect swollen lymph nodes. Now that she has her nursing license, which she acquired, as scheduled, a year and a half into her studies, she can also draw blood when Dr. Davids orders tests. They have a portable centrifuge and a container with dry ice, and she's learned to process the samples. Patients often need help understanding how to take their medicines, and she meets with them to write clear instructions on when to take pills. She draws charts in pen, making lines between the picture of a sun and the picture of a moon, usually drawing a center column, and writing the number of pills in numbers or lines. Many of these people are illiterate, some are brilliant but lost in a world of schizophrenia, sometimes drug-induced, and most are just unemployed and maybe on drugs or alcohol.

Tommy is one of the latter. He tells her he's gone on and off drugs for more than twenty years, but now that he's approaching fifty, his drugs are meeker and he's ready to stop using for good. Although there are injection tracts along his arms, he hasn't used heroin since being diagnosed with HIV two years ago. For a long time, he's been on a waiting list for housing. He's a thin white man, who squints when he talks to her, and his dark brown hair that's pulled back in a ponytail is sprinkled with grey. She's seen him at the van twice already. She talked to him about AA and NA groups, and printed out a copy of where the groups met and when, which she gave to him. He sort of laughed when she did this, but told her he appreciated her concern. His recovery is precarious, because his only real support is the van, Dr. Davids, and the possibility of shelter that has nothing to do with behaving nicely or life being "fair."

Tommy has HIV, but his health is stable. The first time he came to the portable clinic he had bronchitis, and the second time he wanted his blood drawn to "check his numbers."

When they've been at the park about half an hour, she spots him in line, waiting with the other patients. She climbs into the front of the van and looks in the lab folder for his results, and finds them filed under "T." There are five people waiting, and he's at the end of the line. She catches his eye and he waves to her. She walks to where he is.

"Hey Rosie, how you doing?" he says as she approaches.

"Good, good. How about you?"

"I'm fine. Just waiting to talk to the doc."

"Are you here for results?" She asks this quietly, so others won't suspect his status. He nods his head. She shows him that she has them in her hand. "We can go over them, if you'd like."

He follows her to the other side of the van, where no one is waiting and where the sound of traffic on the other side will drown out anything they have to say. She and Dr. Davids set up two folding chairs, so she has a place to counsel patients or review blood work results, as she will with Tommy. They sit, and she holds the paper so that he can see the numbers that she's referring to.

"It actually looks pretty good," she tells him. "Your CD4, which will help you fight disease, is 374, and your viral load is 43,000."

"Is that good?" he asks.

"Well, ideally we'd like to have it undetectable." The test measure down to 400 copies of virus, so they can never say it's zero, they can only tell patients that the test can't find it, and the virus is therefore "undetectable."

Tommy nods. "That means starting medication, right?"

"Yes. But the medicines are getting better, and easier to take."

"I don't want to be taking no 50 pills a day."

"You probably won't have to."

"Probably?"

This is the part of talking to patients that's difficult for Rosie. She doesn't know what she can promise. She envies the doctors and nurse practitioners giving information with confidence.

"Honestly," she takes a deep breath and sighs. "I don't think so. There's a new drug out, and other older ones that can be given twice a day."

Tommy nods, looking serious. "Will I look like I have HIV?"

"You mean the lipodystrophy changes?" Rosie asks.

"If that means the skinny arms and legs, fat stomach, and sunken cheeks, then yeah, those."

"It's possible," Rosie says, again, frustrated with her lack of knowledge. "I don't think we know much about that yet—like, how it's caused and how to stop it."

"I wish," he looks up at the sky, now beginning to turn to dusk. "I mean, I know how I got this, and I know it was from the drug use, but, if only I could turn back and start again, you know?" It's tragic, and although Rosie hasn't had much experience practicing HIV care, she's heard this before. Ironically, relapse sometimes follows.

"You can't change your mistakes," she says. She thinks of Octavius, and draws on the wisdom that he imbibed in her. "You can only go forward, and not repeat what you've done before. Like, your hepatitis C and B tests came back negative. You can keep them that way."

Tommy rests his elbows on his knees and turns his head to look at her. He sort of smiles and nods his head. "So does the doc want me on meds?"

Rosie's relieved that at last she has a definite answer, since she and Dr. Davids had gone over these results and he had prepped her for this conversation. "He says you're close, but it's not entirely necessary right now. If you really wanted to start, you could, but you don't have to."

"Well," he sits back again. "I should have housing next month. I'd like to wait until then."

"I think that's fine," she tells him. Dr. Davids has come around the van, looking for her.

"Hey doc!" Tommy jumps up to shake his hand.

"Hi Tommy, how are you?" They talk about the blood work results and, to Rosie's relief, he reiterates what she had told him. She watches the conversation, and is impressed by the mutual respect and admiration as well as Tommy's gratitude. He shakes his hand again at the end of their brief visit, and Tommy says, "I can't thank you enough, doc. Just being here, and helping me stay clean. It's changed my life."

"My pleasure," he says, and turns to Rosie to show her the blood tests he wants on the patient waiting in the van.

Three weeks later, on a Friday night, Rosie takes a cab with her two roommates to a bar downtown. She wears a short black skirt and a purple shirt with a wide neck, revealing the curve of her collar bone. She wears black nylons and two and a half inch black stilettos to elevate her from her five foot two inch height. As they wait to get into the club she shivers in the night's cold air. When the breeze blows, the cold rakes further toward her core. Down the street, less than a block away, homeless people curl under newspapers in doorways that offer about two feet of shelter from the wind, the night, and the pedestrians carelessly drifting by. She thinks of Tommy, briefly, then turns her attention back to her friends and the man working the door, looking at I.D.s then handing them back while staring blankly past them, bored or irritated. After half an hour, they're inside. She orders margaritas, and after two of them, she starts to feel the weightless, spinning feeling that alcohol gives her. They've met two classmates, and they crowd around a small table, telling stories, laughing, and toasting with each round and in between when a point is made.

Rosie gets up to get another drink and steadies herself before walking to the bar. She stands next to an attractive man with dark hair and a black shirt, and smiles shyly when he turns toward her. They strike up a conversation, about the bar, the city, how long they've lived here and where they're from. He's an attorney, he says, and he's articulate with a gorgeous smile that makes her blush. He buys her a drink.

"My name's Evan," he extends a hand.

"Rosie," she blushes when he continues to hold it, and she notices that his eyes are a little red, and he's also a little unsteady on his feet.

"What's your middle name?"

"Rose." She giggles.

"So . . . Rosie Rose?" they both laugh.

"No, my first name is Domenica. My Grandmother's name was Rose and my family always just called me Rosie."

"Domenica Rose." His voice is like a song. She listens to him tell a story about how this bar was opened and the pictures on the walls. It's loud enough that he has to talk into her ear. The bar tender has walked by twice. She smiles and her heart is pounding as he moves away from her ear and then toward her to kiss her. The intoxication is fabulous. She feels as though she's absolutely floating and wishes for the entire bar to disappear so that she can get even closer to him. She takes half a step toward him and their bodies are almost touching. The voices hum around them and there's music lost behind it. She's hypnotized by it, and shifting her weight on her other foot, she grabs hold of his arm to keep from falling.

"Last call," the bar tender shouts out. A few minutes later, her roommate is tapping on her shoulder and saying into her ear, hey, cupid, Jess called for the cab, then she winks at her and walks back to their table.

"Domenica Rose, would you like to have coffee with me, sometime?" he asks into her ear. Rosie smiles and nods. She tells him her phone number and he pulls out a cell phone to enter it. He asks her twice, repeating the numbers incorrectly the first time. The lights will turn on soon, and her roommate's are coming toward her again. She turns to go. When she turns back to wave, he's already gone.

All week, she hurries home to check the messages on their answering machine. She feels nervous when one of her roommates picks up the phone to make a call, and is distracted by their conversation, relaxing only slightly when the phone is placed back on the receiver. They tell her things like, "meant to be" and "do you really want to meet the love of your life in a bar?" and things about "fish in the sea" when she whines about it on Thursday. By Saturday she begins to lose hope. Another week goes by and she feels her desperation. She runs her finger down the lists of attorneys in the yellow pages of the phone book. Her roommates get an action figure doll and leave it half naked on her bed to cheer her up. She laughs when she see it, but by then it's been more than two weeks, and her laughter turns into tears of frustration. She wipes at her tears and lies down on the bed and looks toward the window. Outside there is nothing. Not even the moon.

Two months and Christmas and New Year's go by. Her family comes to celebrate the holidays with her. Her Italian mother and father both shed tears when they see her and when they say good-bye. She admires her five foot tall mother prancing through the airport to hug her, arms open wide, in heels almost an inch higher than her own, her hair died a reddish brown, her smile authentic and huge. Her father, graying, with black and white slicked back hair, limps behind her, carrying a suitcase almost as big as her mother. She returns to class and her clinical assignments feeling refreshed, and also excited that this semester is her last.

Her clinical with Dr. Davids will extend, and she'll spend another day once a week with a nurse practitioner who works at the University. She looks forward to the day in Dr. Davids clinic, where the scattered journals are familiar and she doesn't have to ask where anything is in the exam room.

Two weeks into the semester, at the end of the day, she sees Tommy in the waiting room. It's odd to see him in an enclosed room, and she notices that the color of his face is wrong. He's pale, and his brow is furrowed with lines of sweat on the sides of his face. He's holding his right foot, and rocking back and forth. Her first thought is a broken toe. She takes his chart and leads him back to an exam room.

"Hi Tommy," he barely looks at her, and nods his head. She helps him onto the exam table. "What's going on with your foot?"

"It hurts, Rosie." Tears squeeze out of his eyes. She takes his temperature. 103. Could he have something else, too? Pneumonia? The flu? She checks it again. 103.4. Looking in the chart, she notes that he's been taking HIV medicine for more than a month, since he obtained permanent housing. His last visit was two weeks ago, and his laboratory results from that visit are all normal, with his viral load already on a sharp downward trend.

"It got infected—you know, an ingrown toenail, and I was soaking it every day for the past week or so." She nods, taking his blood pressure. 100/54. Low. She's seen sick patients with Dr. Davids and knows that their blood pressure drops with serious infections. Tommy takes off his dirty sock, holding his breath, shaking, and sweating profusely as it tumbles off and he moans and lies back on the grey table, throwing an arm over his clenched closed eyes.

"I couldn't even put my shoe on . . ." breathing fast "it hurt so bad." She looks and her own breath stops. His toe is white and she knows before she touches it that it's cold; she's looking at dead flesh. Above the big toe, on his right foot, his skin is scarlet and hot, and there's a red line extending up his foot from here. The flesh above it, the curling black hairs on his skin, looks so alive in comparison.

"When did the fever start?" She asks.

"This morning."

"Okay, okay." She says distractedly, trying to hide the panic. Turning to the sink, she washes her hands and rubs alcohol gel on them as well. Tommy puts his elbows down and rocks himself up. His eyes are rimmed with red and his hair is sticking to the sides of his head. She reaches for the door, looks him in the eye and tells him, "I'll be right back."

She rushes down the hall and knocks on the door of the exam room where she knows Dr. Davids is seeing another patient. She stares into the dark brown wood of the door, willing herself not to open it without his answer. "Yes?" the even sound of his voice calms her. She opens the door.

"Excuse me," she smiles at the patient, then turns to Dr. Davids. "I need you." Her voice is uneven again and her adrenaline racing to all the cells of her body.

"Excuse me for a moment, Bill." Dr. Davids steps into the hall. "Whatta you got?"

"Tommy's here, you're familiar with him, right?" he nods. "Sure. I saw him recently after he started on meds. He's doing quite well with them as I recall." Rosie nods in agreement. She explains, "He's had an infection in his foot for more than a week, then fevers starting today." She reads off his vital signs; high fever, rapid pulse, low blood pressure. She describes Tommy's foot. "I think it's nec fasc." Necrotising fasciitis: "flesh-eating bacteria." It's a condition that killed one of Dr. Davids' patients five years before she met him. The case had affected him so profoundly, that he discusses the signs of it the first day of their assignment. There have been medical students rotating through the clinic, and she's heard his explanation of it often enough, she can recite it herself. The fever, the degree of pain, the color and eerily cold feel of the skin, all stick in her memory without her needing to refer to notes or textbooks.

Dr. Davids looks concerned. "Let's take a look." He strides down the hall to where Tommy still sits, rocking with pain.

The ambulance arrives almost immediately, and Dr. Davids calls the ER attending, the podiatrist, and the surgeon who's successfully worked on these types of cases before. A team is assembled and Tommy is prepped for the OR as soon as he arrives at the hospital. At the clinic, Dr. Davids finishes seeing his patients and then prepares to go to the hospital, where he has privileges and sees his hospitalized patients. He packs his brown, weathered briefcase and puts on the white coat that he wears at the hospital when doing rounds. He goes to the closet in his office and finds an extra one while Rosie finishes a note in the chart. She looks up to see him extending the garment to her.

"Coming?" he asks. She puts down the chart.

In the car, on the way there, neither of them speak, the focus on the street in front of them and the situation the drive will lead them to. When they are almost there, he states, as if in mid-conversation, "I think he'll be okay." She doesn't answer, but nods. "They'll be able to save his leg." He pauses. They wait at a red light. It turns green and they begin to move. A few minutes later he continues, "But it's early enough that . . . .." he trails off and there's once again silence. She looks at him, expecting the completion of this thought. He negotiates the car into a space in the parking garage.

That night, she can't sleep. Her eyes won't even stay closed long enough for her to feel her exhaustion. She looks at the clock. 12:54. She tosses off the covers and shuffles to the kitchen to put on some water for tea.

The events of the day spiral through her mind. She sees Tommy's taught face in the waiting room, his foot, and then the sight of his body, relaxed and sedated in the OR. She still hears the discussion with the surgeon that Dr. Davids had before the procedure, and his invitation for them both to scrub in, with his nod toward her. The feel of the soap is still on her arms and forearms, and her eyes can still see the expert movements of the podiatrist and surgeon, removing the infected toe and filleting the skin above Tommy's foot to look for healthy tissue. She thinks of the monitor, and how she glanced at the numbers to see that they were stable. The antibiotics dripped in, following Dr. Davids' instruction, and she waited with him in the recovery area, to explain to Tommy what had transpired. A sister appeared in the waiting room, and Rosie had talked to her about the operation, carefully avoiding any other disclosure about Tommy's health. She sips her tea, now, and smiles again as she recalls how Dr. Davids looked her in the eye and said "good job, Rosie. Good catch." For the first time since beginning school, she feels a sense of accomplishment and the confidence that she can do this, she can succeed in this career. The feeling of being part of a team that saved a person's life is exhilarating.

She holds her cup of tea in its ceramic mug and stands by the living room window. The street is quiet. Wet, cool, Bay air seeps through the cracks of the windows and seemingly even the walls. The glow of city lights illuminates the sky. She remembers the dark, dark nights in Africa when they could see stars all around and how she and Octavius lay on their backs on the roof, talking and looking for shooting stars. The night was endless then, and felt complete, but she had an almost adolescent angst about the future before her. Octavius had said to her, this IS the future. She sighs. She thinks of Art and realizes she hasn't talked to him in months. It seems odd that they would remain so close, despite long lapses between conversations. Their friendship is like a light shining through a window. There are periods of time that are like drapes pulled across this window, obstructing the transfer of light. As soon as the heavy fabric is moved, there is the continuity of light, glowing naturally through space and oblivious to time. When she calls him, it will be as though the shades are once again opened. Light pouring in and always making her smile. Their connection is strong. In less than five months, she'll graduate, sit for boards, and be a nurse practitioner. She can go anywhere, then. Excitement bubbles within her. Today, tonight, she feels like she could fly to where ever this is herself. The insides of her shoulder blades itch with wings, ready to unfurl.

She finishes her tea, and finally her thoughts have slowed so that her eyelids feel heavy. She rinses the mug and treads quietly back to bed. As she pulls up the covers, it occurs to her that she never asked what kind of law Evan practiced. She wonders if she would recognize him if she saw him on the street or in the subway. Sighing, she admits that she finally doesn't care. She falls asleep easily, dreaming of the tops of mountains hovering between the ocean and the sky.

Riding home after her last day of finals, the city looks brand new. Since arriving here, she's been entirely focused on school, and the reality that she's done with classes and clinicals has begun to sink in as she pedals home. Her elation on August 10th when she turned in her final last exam leads her to detour significantly before going home. She rides across the Golden Gate Bridge, then turns left to climb a winding road to the top of an overlook where, on a clear day, the city is like a postcard. It's not as clear as today, but pausing to look at the bay she drinks from her water bottle and thinks it's perfect. She rides down like she's flying, and stands on the pedals to feel the air. The last hills to her apartment are harder than usual, but in a satisfying way. She locks her bike to the inside of the gate, and takes her time climbing the steps to the apartment.

On the kitchen table, she finds a package waiting for her. She checks the return address: Denver, Colorado. She smiles as she rips open the package to find a card and a copy of Dr. Seuss' *Oh, the Places You'll Go*. She reads his words. "Congratulations, Rosie, NP! How about Colorado, next?" She goes to sit at the computer, gets online, and checks the *Denver Post* classified again. It's still there.

He answers his cell phone with, "So, I have this pain in my right knee . , ,."

"Art! I don't take the boards for another two months! And then there's malpractice, ..."

"Come on, you know I'd never sue!"

She laughs and walks over to the coach, where she collapses. "So how are you?"

"Good. It's a beautiful day here in sunny Colorado."

"Yeah? Well, it's not bad here, but it's getting cooler now."

"Hm."

"Thanks for the book!"

"You're welcome. I hope you don't have it already."

"No, I stopped collecting Seuss when I was about seven."

"Very funny."

"Seriously, it was really great of you to send it. It got here today, you know—right when I got home from taking my last exam."

"Great! Thanks for your e-mail that clued me in on when to send it."

They talk about their lives, his teaching job at a public high school, which he loves to hate, and relationships. She gazes out the window, relaxing and enjoying a conversation where there's no multiple choice right answer. Finally, she says to him, "So, there's this job I'm thinking of applying for . . .."

The end of August comes, after graduation with assorted celebrations with family, friends, and her friends' families. In less than a week, she'll leave for Colorado, having completed a phone interview for the job she applied for. It's in the infection control department, but overlaps with infectious disease since there's a need for an RN within that clinic. It's not perfect, and not entirely what she envisioned, but it could be a stepping stone to something else. When the supervisor called and offered her the job, she accepted.

She examines herself in the mirror, evaluating the green shirt with black pants that she's chosen to wear to this luncheon. Dr. Davids has invited her, and when he told her his son would join them, she felt relief. After almost a year of knowing Dr. Davids, she still can't have a comfortable conversation with him. The pictures of happy children in his office convince her that the son will relieve this tension.

Still, she's pulled out four shirts and three pairs of pants before deciding what to wear. She wishes for Octavius' eye for fashion. He was still the most impeccable dresser she's ever met. She pulls the shirt down to straighten it once more and glances at the clock. Without any more time to agonize over her wardrobe, she collects her wallet and purse and heads out the door.

The café is crowded when she arrives. She's early, which is uncomfortable, but doesn't make her feel as guilty as being late. There aren't that many tables and it's easy to see that she's the first to arrive. She gives her name to the maitre d' and turns to see Dr. Davids walking down the sidewalk. He gives her a hug, which feels unfamiliar but fatherly. He carries a large purple bag which he hands to her. It's heavy and she immediately knows it's a reference book.

"Congratulations on your graduation," he says.

"Thanks." She tries to hold the bag with one hand so she can reach into it, but it's too heavy. She holds it against her and awkwardly pulls the bag down to reveal the title. "Wow! This is great!" It's a book on the medical management of infectious disease that she frequently looked at in his office and that he would refer to, as well, when treating patients. She thinks of when she'll use it, and she's aware of a sinking feeling that pulls at her when she thinks of her upcoming interview. She can't envision using any sort of reference such as this while working as a nurse in a clinic or in infection control administration.

"It's been a pleasure to work with you. You'll be a great nurse practitioner."

She smiles at him. "Thank you."

Their conversation is interrupted by the maitre d', who leads them to a table toward the back. Dr. Davids tells her about the clinic, and his hope to expand within the next few years. For the first time, he mentions retirement, and his desire to decrease his workload. They peruse the menu, and before she can decide her choice, his son strides in and Dr. Davids stands to embrace him.

For a moment, she can't move. Although she knows the pictures in his office are old, she never thought about them enough to realize that the toddler would be a grown man, with deep brown eyes, a muscular build, and a stunning smile. The confidence that she'd had that conversation would be easier is gone. He reaches his hand toward her. She rises and shakes his hand, as Dr. Davids introduces his son, Trey. He covers her hand with his left and smiles broadly, saying how much he's heard about her and assuring her it's all positive.

The café is Trey's choice, and he barely glances at the menu to decide what to order. He's easy to talk to, and she recognizes Dr. Davids' ability to listen and empathize as she speaks. He's a physical therapist and works in Oakland, but he lives in the city, not far from his parents. She tells them both about her possible move east, and they both are encouraging about moving to Colorado. The food arrives, and the conversation flows. Dr. Davids' softer, paternal side unveils, and she admires the relationship of father and son. Trey asks him about the clinic, telling him he looks tired and asking him about his next vacation, reminding him of his last, suggesting that two hands to count years between vacations is two many. He tells Rosie about their trip to Tahoe, and of Dr. Davids' adventure in mistakenly turning down a black diamond trail. She laughs with them and it feels like family.

"Do you ski?" Trey asks her.

"No. I never had an opportunity to learn. We moved to Florida when I was in junior high school, and the thing to do there was surf."

"Did you do that?"

"A little."

"Well, you could try snow boarding." She sees Dr. Davids frown. "Come on, Dad!" he playfully slaps his arm. "They're not all bad!" He takes a sips of ice water, looks toward her, and winks. His left hand is bare of jewelry. Her car is half loaded already. "Timing," she thinks, and smiles back.

October 2000

The darkness comes early, since the mountains block the sun. The match hisses, alive with flame as she arches it over to the candle's wick. Uniting stick and wax she waits for the glow of established fire before removing the match and shaking it out. Looking into the flame, she remembers, trying hard not to miss the roar of the ocean, the taste and feel of salt in the air, and the smell of eucalyptus she longs for. She tries not to miss her friend, even though it is for him she's lit this flame. She attempts to forgive her oversight; late in the afternoon she looked at the calendar and realized what she had forgotten. Her eyes hurt from the contrast between bright flame and surrounding darkness, but still she looks. She remembers. She cries this time for him and for herself and the miserable life she's flailing into. Her life resembles a misstep from a winding path on the steep side of a mountain, and now her feet are skidding on scree. She's barely upright and beginning to doubt the continuation of a path below. A sob and she covers both eyes with both hands and squeezes the emotions away. She shudders. Maybe tomorrow will be better, she thinks, and distinguishes the light with a quick exhalation.

December 2000

She's awake. Staring at the popcorn ceiling, trying to find shapes
in the lumps that hang down. Without thinking she moves to wipe her
sleepy eyes, but she's stopped by the pain in her upper arm when she lifts
her right forearm three inches from the futon. She has to pee but getting
up, no, that's too much. Lying on her back staring takes the least energy
and causes the least pain, so she's happy not to move. It's the morning
after her first day of attempting to snowboard. She'd slept in the spare
room, stretched out on the futon that covered almost half of the floor,
waking with pain every time she'd tried to adjust her position to one more
comfortable, even as the stiffness and true soreness tunneled in. She'd
practically crawled to the bathroom at midnight, finding her way in the
unfamiliar condo by memory and feel, then carefully crumpled back to
bed. When she awoke an hour ago, she'd tried to get up, but sitting was
torture so she didn't want to increase the pain by standing. She lay back
on the pillow. For an hour, she lay looking for shapes and thinking, and
her mind kept snaking back to her job.

"Job." The full history of the word makes her want to laugh at
the irony, but she's just so tired of her employment that the humor has

disintegrated into ashes of disappointment and spent rage. Why did she leave the city that she loved?, she wonders. For what?

The first few weeks were just overwhelming and new. Her days were saturated with learning: the clinics, the different hospital floor specialties, the cafeteria, the bathrooms, and the location of the best coffee. The first co-workers seemed all right, not spectacular or potential best friends, but not terrible to work with. The nurse in infection control, Maggie, was cordial, and briefed her on projects and statistics in the hospital. The paperwork was dreary and the data entry less than challenging. The conversations with Maggie approached the same level. But in addition to her position in infection control, two days a week in the clinic there was Amelia. Amelia made Rosie look forward to Maggie and the paperwork.

In the clinic, Amelia's dominance mentally led Rosie back to her first injection as a student. Providing clinical support involved many tasks Rosie had no experience in; hanging medicine made her nervous, drawing blood when medical assistants failed was almost impossible, and starting IV's daunted her. Three weeks into the job, Amelia instructed her to start an IV on a patient who was dehydrated and needed a liter of fluid. Rosie introduced herself, expressing sympathy with his current illness. She assured him hydration would help, telling him about electrolytes while he stared at the ceiling, periodically closing his eyes. She found a vein, cleaned the skin, and held her breath when she pushed in the catheterized needle. She was accustomed to injections and blood draws, though, when only a smooth needle enters and there's little resistance from the skin. Her push with the catheterized needle was too slow, and he recoiled his arm, shouting "BITCH!". He snapped his other arm down and attempted to grab the needle from her, yelling, "how 'bout I stab you like that, hunh?!" as she sprang back, shocked. The extent of his assault, since he had HIV, didn't even register with her that moment. Rosie mumbled, "Sorry," placed the needle in the sharps container, and tossed her gloves in to the trash on the way out of the procedure room. She stopped at the clean holdings closet and found an unopened IV kit. Amelia asked, "How did it go?" when Rosie knocked on her open office door. She did not return Rosie's smile as she handed her a new kit, explaining her failure and the patient's response. Amelia told her to toughen up, but heaved her 200 plus pound frame out of the chair, looked longingly at her half eaten doughnut, then stomped into the procedure room. Rosie did not follow. She'd sighed, looked at the ceiling, and said to herself, maybe it'll get better. One of the Fellows had walked by briskly, his long white coat splayed out behind him like a superhero's. She stepped out of the way.

She thinks of this now, as she stares at the condo ceiling, noticing a pattern of lumps that slightly resembles a giraffe. The image disappears when she looks away for a moment, and she can't find it again. Her body continues to hurt. Outside, snow is falling. Fat flakes float down and the view of the mountains fades in the low heavy clouds. She has no desire to ride a chair lift ever again. Her tailbone probably aches the most, where she had landed after dismounting a chair. Coccyx, she thinks, and wonders how to tell if it's broken. The lifts had stopped as the operator waited for her to roll, hop, and limp out of the way, with Jenny on one side of her and Art on the other, guiding and pulling her along.

"Do you think she's awake?" Rosie hears a quiet voice ask outside of her room.

"It's almost 10:00, she's gotta be!" Art's voice answers.

"Should we go in?"

"I dunno. I figured she'd come out by now."

"So maybe she *is* asleep?" Rosie can picture Jenny's hesitant expression.

"Why don't you knock on the door." It's really more of an order than a suggestion.

Rosie hears a clock tick. Strange, she thinks, because she hadn't noticed it before.

"She's really *your* friend. You do it!" The comment makes Rosie wonder if Jenny has befriended her only out of obligation.

"Yeah, but you have that female to female understanding." Jenny giggles and Rosie imagines them poking each other as Art laughs, and then Jenny utters a half shriek followed by "SSHHHHHHH!" A few moments pass.

"Okay," Jenny says. "But I'm not going in unarmed. You get the coffee, okay?"

"Roger." There's the faint sound of a kiss and footsteps retreating, then returning after a pause in the vicinity of the kitchen. A soft knock on the door, "Rosie?"

"Yeah! Come in." She's looking forward to the coffee.

Jenny steps in. "How are you feeling?"

"I can't move." Jenny sits down on the edge of the futon, looking sympathetic as she holds the coffee toward her, but stops, not sure how to give it to her while she's recumbent. She looks around the room, then decides to put the coffee on the floor.

"Here," she positions herself to help Rosie sit up. "I'll help you."

With a few movements and grimaces, Rosie is sitting up, afraid to think about how she must look with her hair matted and eyes still tired and a little red. "Thanks." Jenny hands her the coffee. "Did you sleep okay?"

"Yeah, I'm just sore from yesterday."

"Learning's hard, but it's fun once you get the hang of it!" Rosie forces a smile. "So you don't want to try again today?" Rosie laughs. She's amazed that in a sea of people, Art and Jenny have managed to find each other; two people who come up with almost exactly the same sarcastic remarks. "No, I don't think so." The door is ajar and Art pokes his way in.

"Hey! How's it goin' in here?" He leans against the doorframe. Jenny has somehow convinced him finally to have his hair cut stylishly, and his glasses are actually very hip. Rosie's happy for them and a little jealous as she watches the way Jenny smiles up at him now.

"Mornin'" Rosie tells him.

"We were just discussing the fun of learning how to snowboard."

"Yeah, I remember those days. A little sore today?"

"Understatement." She holds the coffee in both hands. Even the act of raising it to her lips is uncomfortable.

"So you don't want to go up with us today?"

Jenny and Rosie exchange looks.

Art cranes his head to get a better look out the window. "Looks like a little bit of powder up there."

"Hmm." Rosie feels depressed.

Rosie finally agrees that getting up is inevitable, especially since she's drinking coffee. She hands the cup to Art. Jenny helps her stand, her quads balking as she feebly rises. They meet in the living room, Rosie still in her pajamas but feeling just a bit more human having washed her face, brushed her teeth, and arranged her hair. She falls into the couch.

"Bagel?" Art asks across the low counter, holding it up in the air to show her. The TV is on and Jenny sits in an armchair, watching it but appearing to think of something else.

"Yes, please!" Rosie replies. She smells it toasting and realizes she's hungry. Art comes in with a glass of water and the bagel on a plate, slathered with cream cheese.

"You need to re-hydrate and flush out that lactic acid."

"Yes, Dr. Art," Rosie teases him.

"Ooo, I like that!" Jenny winks at him. He deposits three ibuprofen on the coffee table in front of Rosie, then moves to where Jenny sits. They kiss and Rosie concentrates on the TV. He leans on the arm of Jenny's chair.

"Do you mind if Jenny and I go do a few runs? We won't be long—we still want to hit the road by, say two."

"No, that's okay. You should go after having to spend half the day yesterday scooping me up out of the snow."

"It wasn't that bad!" Jenny tells her. "I think you were starting to get it by the end of the day."

"Was that before or after ski patrol had to bring me down?" She refers to the previous day, at its end when the sun had started to set, glowing pink and yellow through the barren trees and reflecting on the snow across the mountaintops. Rosie couldn't do more than flop down the mountain, attempting to stand on tired legs, sliding a few feet, falling forward, backward, or sideways into the snow. When they'd heard the hum of a snow mobile approach, she'd acquiesced to the aid. The assistance was fine, until she'd had to dismount at the bottom of the hill in front of what felt like a hundred people. She self-consciously felt them all turn to watch her stumble off with her snowboard awkwardly stuffed under her arm. Scores of snowsuit clad people with goggles on top of their heads sat outside the bar laughing into drinks and occasionally moving to the beat of music blaring from speakers above. She joined Art and Jenny at a table, not really wanting to stay, but accepting the beer that arrived in front of her.

"You did fine for you first day!" Art assures her as he steps back into the kitchen to rinse his coffee cup. "You about ready?"

Jenny gets up and stretches. She's long and slim; matching Art perfectly. "Yup. You sure you'll be okay?"

"Positive. Have fun."

In another five minutes they're gone, and as the door closes, Rosie wishes she'd begged them to stay. The condo feels lonely, and the Sunday morning TV commercials make her feel worse. She looks at her empty plate and begins to cry. She just feels so tired. Channel surfing for an hour and a half brings her finally to coverage of professional skiing. Disgusted, she turns it off entirely. There are no sounds. She feels the cold empty space of the universe and wonders how she can continue to exist in it. Curling on her side on the couch, she hugs a pillow and waits for them to return, when they can finally leave the mountains.

They ride back down the mountains mostly in silence, listening to music, watching the mountains go by. Rosie's in the back, staring out at the trees and brown, rocky sides of earth. Once they're through the Eisenhower tunnel, there's no new snow. The green pines end in a scant, hard layer of snow and near Georgetown, where the sun hits the side of the mountain, the ground is bare. It takes three and a half hours to return to town, because the heavy ski traffic clogs the highway and gradually slows their speed until they merely stop and go. It's a frustrating ride, but eventually the traffic breaks up east of Idaho Springs. Once in Denver, Art stops in front of her building. She thanks them and hobbles to the door. It's dark, and she flips on the light and opens her refrigerator, looking for something edible that won't involve effort. Unsatisfied, she closes it and moves to the stove, pulling out a saucepan and filling it partly with water. As she breaks the ramen noodles into the boiling water, she's thinking, I should get a cat, maybe. Or a fish. Just so I have someone to come home to. She goes back to the refrigerator and pulls out a beer. She wipes her eyes with the back of her hand, then cracks the can open.

That following week, she limps through her work days taking the elevator instead of the stairs, thinking of every task she can complete while standing so she can limit bending her knees, engaging her quadriceps, and grimacing with the aching pain involved with sitting or standing. She keeps her water bottle with her. Amelia doesn't demonstrate any sympathy, and expresses her general disgust with snowboarding. Maggie, at least, fills her water bottle for her on Monday when it's empty, and offers to get her coffee when she goes to buy her own. Rosie holds it in both hands and thanks her.

After a week, the soreness is gone. Rosie spends the weekend with her books, memorizing pathophysiology, signs and symptoms of disease, and treatment plans in preparation for her nurse practitioner boards. She drinks coffee, plays music, and remembers the days of studying for the NCLEX with her friends. Her focus drifts, and every twenty minutes she needs to take breaks.

She holds the phone to her ear and waits.

"Hello, Rosie Sunshine."

"Hey. How are you?"

"Well my shoulder has this aching feeling. And I think I have chest pain."

"Very funny."

He laughs. "How's the studying?"

"Oh, you know. Studious. I had to take a break, though. There's just so much information."

"I bet. The human body is very complex."

"Mm. What are you guys up to?"

"Hanging out. Not much. But I'm glad you called, 'cause I read this article that made me think of you."

"Oh yeah?"

"Yeah. It's about this study that some psychologists did on performance. They had a bunch of basketball players—"

"I've never played basketball."

"Funny. Keep listening. They divided them into three groups and had one practice, one think about practicing, and one do both. The interesting thing is that the group who practiced and the group who thought about it ended up performing about the same."

"Art, I'm not going snowboarding again."

"I know. I wasn't thinking about that. I was thinking about that IV stuff you were talking about."

"Hm. Yeah. I guess I could apply that." She had told them about her frustrating inability to start an IV.

"And, you know, if you think about snowboarding . . ." she laughs.

Rosie puts her books away when the words stop making sense and her mind can no longer retain what she reads for more than a moment. She feels saturated mentally, and good, as she stands up and realizes her legs no longer ache. She gets a broom to sweep the kitchen and then prepares a meal. She thinks of what Art told her.

As she lies in bed, at the end of the day, she closes her eyes and pictures an IV start kit. She imagines herself opening it, putting on her gloves, and she thinks of the IV. Picturing a patient's arm, she sees in her mind the vein, feeling it with a finger before cleaning the area with alcohol and iodine. Moments pass while it dries. She thinks of the feel and weight of the needle, imagines what she'll say to her patient, and in her mind, deftly slides it in.

The next morning begins with a pink sunrise and Rosie admires the color of the sky as she walks from her building to her car. It feels like a good day, even if it's Monday and work is a chore. She wonders if her mantra, "Maybe tomorrow will be better" will finally come true. Silently she applauds her own patience.

Monday is a clinic day, which always makes the day feel blacker. She routinely orders a double shot in her cappuccino on Monday to jumpstart the day. Caffeine makes her happier. Something about the increased rate of her heart makes her walk as if there's a cushion of air beneath the soles of her feet, even though the rubber soles of her shoes confirm reality with a quiet squeak-slap as she steps. The lights are off in the procedure room when she enters, and she flicks the switch before putting her cup down on a tray table to take inventory. She counts needles and syringes, then walks down the hall to make sure the closet is stocked. Satisfied, she returns to the room and sits on a rolling chair, sipping her drink, absentmindedly pushing the ground with her feet to turn slowly in the chair.

The medical assistant, Terry, has a lot of experience in phlebotomy, and Rosie seldom needs to step in to help her when she fails to draw blood. They put warm packs on patients hands to make the vein pop out, and sometimes have them dangle a purple looking arm after applying the tourniquet and waiting. Rosie learns more than she teaches in the procedure room. She gives testosterone injections and laughs to herself when a patient comes in for his two week shot with the bandaid of the last shot still in place. As she pulls off the old one, she gently reminds him to remove the one she places on his left buttuck at the end of his day. He laughs and thanks her.

At eleven, one of the doctors escorts her patient into the room. "Who's the nurse today?" she asks. The schedule is pretty consistent, but the doctors can't keep it straight.

"Rosie," Terry answers, not looking up from a blood draw, and Rosie approaches the patient.

"Frank, this is Rosie." He nods, looking pale and mumbling "Pleased to meet you."

"Likewise," she says, and, concerned about his coloring, touches his elbow and leads him to the stretcher. "Why don't you lie down here?"

"Thank you," he says, and sighs with gratitude as he reclines.

"Frank needs some fluid to start with, and we'll need some labs." The doctor hands Rosie a lab sheet and she nods, swallowing hard and trying hopelessly not to sweat. The doctor turns to Frank. "I'll be back to check on you in a few minutes."

Rosie collects the equipment she needs for this procedure and arranges it on a rolling table next to the bed.

"I haven't seen you here before. Have you been working here long?"

"About three months," Rosie answers. Frank has a patterned shirt with vivid colors that work together surprisingly to please the eye. She's reminded briefly of Octavius as she notices how he's dressed, from his shirt to the shoes he's wearing.

"Ah. Not long. Well, welcome."

"Thanks." She smiles at him as she ties the tourniquet and slowly turns his arm one way, then the other. His veins are easy to spot, despite his lack of fluids, and she cleans an area of his forearm thoroughly. The gloves are spotted with moisture where her hands have begun to sweat.

She takes the needle with its catheter firmly between her thumb and forefinger. "You've done this before, right?"

"Um hm," Rosie lies, looking down. "Okay, now take a deep breath." Frank obeys. "And blow it out," Rosie herself holds her breath as she moves the needle to his vein and deftly slides the IV in.

She manages to get the blood drawn and the line started without losing the IV, or allowing blood to flow out as she starts the line. Frank leans back with his eyes closed. She adjusts the bed, turns the blood vials to mix the anticoagulant in the container, and places on labels to prepare them for the lab. The medical assistant pats her on the back and winks at her, so Frank can't see her congratulatory wishes.

Elated, Rosie practically runs down the hall, thinking she can finally bond with Amelia, whom she's come to think of as, the Beast. She knocks on her open door.

Amelia violently hurls the chart she was looking at, her pen, and her stack of labs across her desk, "WHAT?!" she roars. The chart slides across Amelia's desk, narrowly missing the framed picture of herself with her partner, Mary, smiling in a grove of aspen.

Rosie feels herself sink, once again joyless. "Nothing. I just got an IV in. I thought I'd tell you." She turns and walks away. Whatever Amelia's response, Rosie can't hear it from the hallway where her own shackles are up and ready for a fight that she instead flees from. The anger has nowhere to go, and it sputters and spirals as she desperately grasps for her next task. She turns into the procedure room and once again evaluates Frank, who is looking more relaxed and less pale. She feels compassion toward him, and eagerly looks around for anything else she can do to make him better quickly. The labs haven't been picked up yet.

"Hey, Terry?"

"Yeah."

"I'm going to bring these down to the lab. Do you have anything else that needs to go?"

Terry closes a ziplock bag with blood vials and hands them to Rosie. "Here you go!"

"I'll be back in a few." But on the way back from the basement, she walks to the hospital entrance and out the door. She stands in the cold, breathing in and blowing out misty breath, smelling the cigarette smoke and noticing that the wind has shifted and the smell of a cattle farm is also in the air. She envisions herself continuing to walk, to her car, her building, her suitcases--to somewhere else where the air is warmer and wetter and, goddamn it, at least smells like air. When she looks around, she sees frail people in coats, overweight people in scrubs, and sagging people in hospital gowns and slippers. They have blankets thrown over their shoulders so they can bear the twenty minutes it takes to suck down the fibers of their cigarettes. They lean on IV poles as they shuffle back through the automatic door. Rosie finally thinks of Frank and steps onto the cement where the doors open, demanding her next move. Forward she goes with a sigh and a shrug, her shoulders rounded into her heart, her head a little lower.

The sidewalks are icy now, and the air is cold. There are only ten days until Christmas, and Rosie doesn't feel like going anywhere, so will stay in Denver for the holiday. She wraps a gift for her mother and father and stands in line at the post office, overheated and sweating as the line slowly moves. She hugs the package to her, suddenly missing her family and wishing she had made plans to visit Florida. There she could walk along the beach without layers of clothing and feel as if Denver were just a bad dream. It's just not clicking yet for you, Jenny had told her. Give it time.

On Thursday she goes to Art and Jenny's after work, bringing eggnog and a bottle of whisky for the party they're preparing. Guests start arriving after six, and Rosie mingles with the few people she's already met; some co-workers of Jenny, an old roommate of Art's. She's casually talking to Art's former roommate when she notices an attractive tall man with dark hair standing in the kitchen. He looks uncomfortable, his hands stuffed into his pockets, attempting to appear nonchalant with arms forced straight and shoulders raised. Rosie excuses herself and walks over.

"Hi," she extends a hand. "I'm Rosie."

He gratefully retrieves a hand from his pockets, making more movements than necessary, and shakes her hand. "Dan." Rosie offers to get him a beer and when he nods and thanks her she goes to the cooler, retrieves a brown bottle, and brings it back open.

"Thanks. Ah. Winter Ale. Good choice!"

"Seems seasonal." He laughs.

"How do you know the hosts?"

"Actually I met Art almost ten years ago . . ." She's interrupted by Jenny, who exclaims, "Dan!" and hugs him. A woman with light brown highlighted hair stands next to her.

"Hey, Jenny." He spills a little of his beer as he rettrieves his arms after the hug. "Thanks for inviting me." He looks around. "Cool place."

"Thanks. Glad you could finally see it!" Rosie tries not to feel irritated by the intrusion. "I'd like you to meet Susan. She's in the physics department at NREL."

"At where?" Rosie asks.

"National Renewable Energy Laboratory." Dan tells her. "Cool. I'm teaching physics at CU, right now."

"Oh, yeah, I think we had an intern from your department." Susan begins to describe the intern as Rosie examines the tiny white lights strung around the kitchen, thinking of Jenny's impeccable taste which Rosie finds overwhelming in its unnecessary attention to detail. Dan laughs at something Susan says and Jenny has excused herself to welcome another guest. Rosie backs herself out of the conversation.

"Nice to meet you, Rose. Thanks for the beer!" She smiles as she leaves the room. When she turns back she sees Art.

"What's wrong?" he asks her. He's wearing a Santa hat, now, and she takes the end and flips it to the other side.

"Nothing. You looked crooked is all." They laugh together.

"Merry Christmas."

"Ho ho ho!"

Mid-January is warmer than December and Rosie climbs up to the roof to study outside in the sun when the midday air is the warmest. She can see the mountains when she looks up, raising her head and running her fingers along her neck which aches from leaning over. The mountains are a rich blue with white peaks cut against a clear blue sky. She knows Art and Jenny are sliding down the Black Diamond trails as she stares at these young, ragged giants, and she wishes them well, jealous they can play but not of what they're doing.

When the afternoon is just starting to get cooler, she hears footsteps, and she turns to see her neighbor sauntering up the steps.

"Hey Rosie!"

"Hi J.T. How are you?"

He walks over, holding a plastic cup. J.T. graduated from Colorado University the previous spring, and although he's only seven years younger than she, she feels as if she could be his mother. "Great! What are you up to?"

"Studying."

He looks at her book. "For what?"

"Nurse practitioner boards."

"Oh. I have an aunt who does that. She's out on the Western slope. Seems to like it. I think she has her own practice now with another NP."

"That's awesome."

"So are you, like, working as an NP? You're at the hospital, right?"

"Yes. I mean no." She shakes her head to clear the words. "I work at the hospital but not as an NP."

"Oh." He takes a drink from his cup. "So we're having a party tonight. Sort of a post-Happy New Year's. You should come by for a beer."

"Okay. What time? Do you need anything?"

"About eight or so. We got a keg, so just bring a cup."

"Okay. Thanks!"

He gazes out at the mountains. "Nice view, hunh?" The sun is just starting to set, and the sky is changing color. Rosie looks west, too. "Yeah."

On Sunday, she calls Art.

"How are you? Did you have fun up in the mountains at the condo?"

"Well, I have this pain in my leg."

"Art, enough with the joint pain jokes."

"No, seriously, Rosie. I jammed my ski into a hole an snapped my lower leg."

Rosie sits down. "You're kidding. I mean, no you're not kidding, but, ow! What happened? Did they set it there?"

"Yeah, I got the ambulance ride to the local hospital and have to see an orthopedist here, tomorrow. Fortunately, it doesn't look like it will need a pin or anything. I just have to stay off of it for awhile."

"That sucks. Right in the middle of the season."

"Yup." She hears him take a sip of something and say "thanks, hon."" She imagines Jenny delivering a hot cup of tea and disappearing again into the kitchen.

"I'm sorry. Well, is there anything you need? I guess Jenny will take care of stuff, but, anything else?"

"Yeah, she's pretty amazing. I'm a terrible patient and she's been great. She's got a conference next week in San Antonio, so I might take you up on your offer then."

"Sure. Anything I can do."

"So how was your weekend?"

She tells him about the party at her neighbors' and how watching the keg stands had made her feel hopelessly old. She describes the jello shots and the mistle toe she had avoided. Many of the guests she had met were still in college, and those who had graduated had temporary positions, just to pay rent and bills. She had only stayed about an hour, and slipped out without notice.

On the third Saturday in January, she drives to the testing center, breathing deeply as she turns from her vehicle to walk purposefully through the doors. The sun is strong, again, but the wind makes her hug her jacket tightly.

The nurse practitioner boards are just as stressful as the NCLEX, making her sweat and blink hard and readjust herself frequently in her chair. But she feels better prepared, having completed her clinicals at school; she can lean on the mental images of patient's faces and medical conditions she'd helped to treat. Her confidence has increased with her clinical experience, so her multiple choice answers feel better directed and more secure.

When she leaves to drive home, she's relieved. As she enters her apartment, she sees her test preparation books and collects them happily to shove them to the nether most regions of her closet. She looks around, trying to determine how to spend this happy energy. She dials the phone.

"Hey Honey!" Richard answers and she can see his smile. She smiles, too, suddenly wishing she were in San Francisco with him. For moral support, they had agreed to visit the testing center on the same day.

"How did it go for you?"

"Good. I think I did okay. It was harder than I thought! How 'bout you?"

"Uh—it's over!! I just hope I passed."

"Yeah, me too. So what are you doing to celebrate?"

"Dunno."

"You're kidding. We've been planning a party for weeks." Richard refers to his new partner, Ken, whom he's been with for six months. "Why don't you call that friend of yours, what's his name? The cute one?"

"Art. Yeah, I guess I could see what he's up to."

She hears a disgusted sigh on the other end. "You know, if you two were gay you'd be sleeping together already!"

"Richard, he's practically engaged!"

"Okay, whatever you say."

"So you're going to have a party?"

After she hangs up the phone, she feels an intense emptiness around her. To edge out the silence, she drums her fingers on the table. Jenny's out of town and calling Art every day while she's gone seems strange. She'd brought him pizza on Thursday and talked to him last night. Still, he'd said to let him know about the boards. Before she can hedge back to deciding not to, she dials his number.

"Did you pass?"

"Won't know for two weeks. But I'm glad it's over!"

"Yay for you! Time to celebrate!"

"I was considering that myself. I just wish I knew more people in town to celebrate with."

"One's enough. Come on over. I'm just sitting here with my foot up!"

She stops at the liquor store on the way and buys a six-pack of beer. Twisting her keys around, she knocks on the door, then finds the one marked "A & J" to let herself in. "Hello!" she shouts as she enters, walking to the fridge with the beer. "Hello!" his muffled voice comes from the other side of the house. Taking her coat off as she walks through the dining room and into the living room, she finds Art reclining with his foot up.

"Don't get up, really," she teases him since he's only raised an index finger to welcome her in.

"Doctor's orders. Must elevate!"

"Hm. What are you watching?" Rosie sits on the couch and looks toward the TV.

"Nothing, really." He clicks it off and leans forward. "Okay Rosie, NP—"

"Maybe."

"Uh." He rolls his eyes. "Okay, soon-to-be Rosie, NP, what do you want to do this historic day?"

"I don't know. Dinner, maybe? You're probably ready to get out of the house."

"What makes you say that?"

"Um, flannel pajama bottoms, a t-shirt with holes, and your ancient hoody." He pulls the scraggly navy blue hood over his head as she talks, making her laugh. "How's Jenny doing at her conference, did you talk to her today?"

"Okay. I think she needed a break from being my caretaker. She says the conference is interesting. There's some guy there she used to date."

"Ah. I brought beer, do you want one?" Rosie points toward the kitchen.

"It took you this long to ask?" She salutes him and jogs through the dining room.

"Show off," he says.

Art emerges from the shower with crutches and faded blue jeans he's cut to fit his cast. He wears a deep green sweater which brings out the flecks of green in his eyes, and she wonders how she missed seeing this color before. They put on their jackets and she drives to a nearby Italian restaurant with a welcoming name. It's cozy, but not romantic, and when they order a bottle of wine, the intimacy feels appropriate. Rosie looks around at the other tables, seeing a few couples and a long table surrounded by ten or so people. She watches as an infant who looks about six months old is passed from one side to the other, wiggling his feet and smiling in a red shirt with over-alls.

"Do you think you'll have kids?" she blurts out.

"Hunh?" Art puts the back of his hand to his mouth as his eyes water.

"You didn't just snort your wine, did you?"

"Well, out of the blue—'do you think you'll have kids'?"

"Do you?"

"Eventually." He follows her gaze to the baby laughing at the rattle before his face. "Oh. I see. Why are all women like that?"

Rosie shrugs. "Hormones, little girl fantasies. According to the five year old me, I'm supposed to be married with three kids right now."

"How much do you really know about life when you're five?" He stares into the menu.

Rosie looks at him thoughtfully. The waiter interrupts them and they order their food.

"Do you want to start with the antipasta?"

Rosie nods. It's an authentic place—red checkered cloth tables, olive oil, music. They order their courses to last the duration of the wine bottle as it gradually empties into their glasses.

110

When Rosie drives Art back to his house, he invites her in. She feels light and giggly from the wine they finished. They each open a beer. She sits next to him on the couch and helps him hoist his foot onto the coffee table. They're laughing, and she doesn't remember why. He twists his arm around behind him to reach for a pillow, struggling to keep his leg balanced. Rosie puts down her bottle. "Here, let me help you." She raises herself on one knee and leans toward him to reach behind him. The proximity is electric; they lock eyes and she freezes, unable to speak. She can smell his aftershave and the wine on his breath as he looks at her, raising an arm to bring her close. They kiss. She leans into him as he pulls her closer and she feels both ecstasy and panic, through momentarily thinking of Jenny her alcohol haze. The thought is gone as her passion rises. Without letting go of each other they move couch cushions and he swivels his leg onto the couch. She longs to be closer to him, to feel her skin on his, in the same moment that he moves his hands under her shirt, on her skin, moving, moving. She pulls her shirt over her head and he grabs at his, tossing clothes aside and lightly shivering the instant they're apart. What they will do is already decided and he pulls a condom from his wallet as she unfastens his jeans and slips off her own.

They lie under Jenny's afghan on the couch, her head on his chest. He's already asleep while she wrenches with guilt. Time passes and she can't sleep, so she untangles herself and dresses. She walks to the kitchen, dizzy, realizing she's probably too drunk to drive home, and probably shouldn't have driven after leaving the restaurant. She can hear Art snoring. "Shit, shit, shit" is all she can think as she repeatedly lightly slaps her forehead. The room is dark, with only the pale illumination of the street light sneaking in and highlighting the outlines of furniture. The refrigerator hums. A car drives by and the headlights zigzag up and down the wall. She touches the back door handle, then turns back. Tiptoeing through the dining room she turns into the hall. She lies down on the bed in the spare bedroom and eventually closes her eyes to sleep. Her dreams are cluttered with faces and colors; songs play through them, loudly, and she wakes with no recollection of what she's dreamt; her head is aching.

The toilet flushes. She hears a thump-shuffle which sounds as if it ends in the kitchen. The clock says 7:38. She gets up.

"Morning." She says to his back. He's shirtless in his jeans reaching for the cereal.

"Hey. I wasn't sure if you were still here."

"I slept in the spare bedroom."

"Excuse me," she moves as he gets a bowl from the cabinet behind where she is standing.

"Um, so, I'm sorry."

"That's okay. I just needed a cereal bowl."

"I mean. About . . . you know."

"It's not like you acted alone." He's pouring his cereal and watching the flakes slide.

"I know, but . . ." she doesn't know how to say she has less to lose.

"But what?"

"I don't know." He hops to the fridge and reaches for the milk. "Are you going to tell her?"

"I hadn't thought about that, yet." He glances at her. "I'm cold. I'm going to go get a shirt." He takes the crutches from where they lean on the table and lurches out.

She sits down at the table in the kitchen. Something inside her makes her want to vacate herself. She wants a shower which will wash away the memory of the night before. Distance, she thinks. The car keys burn in her pocket. Distance, distance, distance. It becomes the rhythm of her heart and the flow of her breath. She wants to run. Her leg is jumping. She doesn't want to see him. He doesn't look at her when he returns to the room.

"I better go." The door closes behind her and she is gone.

A week goes by. Her apartment is dark when she comes home. She starts jogging, just to do something after work which will get her outside and thinking of anything else. It's still too cold and icy for her bicycle. When she's home she looks at the phone, imagines Jenny's face, and mourns their friendship. And Art, whom she misses. Not talking to him makes her job more unbearable, and the absence of their conversations makes her feel there's nothing to laugh about. She stays late at work, entering data, leaving just her desk light on so the office is otherwise dark. The dim lighting and the mindless task comfort her.

Another week begins. On Wednesday, she dips a urine sample to check for infection. While she looks at the second hand of the clock, waiting for the colors to change, she wonders if her mail box will contain her board exam results today. She looks at the stick and squints at the purple, trying to decide what color she sees. Amelia walks by.

"Hey Amelia," she turns and looks at Rosie. "What do you think? Two plus or three plus?" She tilts the stick and the bottle toward her.

"You're kidding me. You don't know how to read a urine dip stick?" Her face is twisted with mockery.

Rosie drops her hands. "Amelia, why did you agree to hire me?"

Amelia is taken aback, yet answers. "You were concentrating on HIV care in school, and I *thought* you were dedicated to it. I thought we were getting someone good, someone we could easily train, someone who . . .". She stops and the pause makes Rosie self-conscious and unsure what to do with her hands or how to plant her feet. She feels vulnerable and inadequate but then realizes something unbelievable and strangely comical. She blurts out without censoring, "Oh, my God. You thought I was gay!" She laughs, shaking her head as she tosses the stick into the red biohazard bag. Amelia's face is red and she begins to stammer a response. Rosie holds up her hand to her, writing down the result of the urinalysis as she continues to smile. She tosses the pen down and walks to Amelia.

"Don't bother. I quit."

"You can't just walk out. You signed a contract agreeing to give two weeks notice!" The Beast is crimson faced and spitting.

Rosie shakes her head, smiling, and turns to go. Under her breath she replies, you signed a contract saying you were an equal opportunity employer. The answer to what she should do is finally clear, and it fills her with relief. She sweeps past Amelia, through the office to collect a few things, and keeps walking.

She parks her car and there's been a dusting of snow during the day. As she walks up the sidewalk, she recalls an iced over puddle she noticed yesterday on her way to go jogging. Just as she wonders, now where is it?, she's slides backwards through the air and lands on her back. The sensation of suddenly looking at the sky startles her, and she doesn't move. It's odd to be going home in the middle of the afternoon; she's not used to daylight at this point of her day. As she lies on her back, she begins to feel the panic of unemployment. She thinks of bills and rent, the fact that she doesn't even know if she's a nurse practitioner yet. Where can she apply? Working on a hospital floor intimidates her, and seems as if it would be more of the same—doing what she doesn't want to do. If this moment feels lonely and the minutes drag by, how will she handle days of it, friendless in a city where she doesn't feel at home? The clouds ease by, dark and light, breaking up and promising a sun that will melt the snow tomorrow. The movement is reassuring. "The only constant thing is change," Octavius had told her as he left Africa. Change, she thinks. She wonders how she can make her life better, since everything seems to be going wrong. She has an irrational anger at the ice; San Francisco doesn't have snow. Neither does Florida. She runs through all the warmer climates she can remember, wishing she could go to each of them, frustrated she can't. In Africa, she had felt stuck after Octavius left, but she'd stayed for the remaining six months, feeling miserable, lonely, and perpetually distracted by Octavius' illness. A hundred times she'd chastised herself for not leaving, wishing she'd had six more months to help him. As she lies in the snow, cold, defeated, and afraid, she suddenly realizes she's been in this moment before. And in this moment, she can leave. I'm free. I can go anywhere, she thinks. The lightness embraces her as she imagines herself in south Florida near her parents, or back in San Francisco, miraculously employed by Dr. Davids and living in the damp, foggy air without the worry of snow or iced puddles. A shadow falls across her.

"You okay?" J. T. is leaning over her, his eyebrows constricted into concern.

"Yeah," she smiles as she takes his hand to be helped up. "I quit my job." The tiny sparkles which float in her vision and her mild dizziness are pleasant.

"Oh." He looks at her imprint in the snow with a confused expression, as if not sure how quitting relates to lying in the snow on the sidewalk. "Well, I'm sorry."

"No, it's a good thing. An opportunity!" He nods without a look of understanding.

"We need to get maintenance out here to put some salt on that ice."

She looks down and shrugs. "It will probably melt tomorrow."

Rosie looks at her watch again. Four o'clock. She continues writing in the chart on her desk. She lists the diagnoses of the patient she had seen and writes the plan as if she were giving cookbook instructions. First, the medicine, then lifestyle changes, blood work to obtain today, and finally dates to return to the clinic. She looks up at the birthday card the office had given her and smiles. In half an hour, Richard and Ken will pick her up to drive down the coast to Moss Beach, where they'll have dinner and watch the sun set. She has one more patient to see, and is relieved the schedule indicates he has sinusitis, which means she won't be stuck trying to manage a complicated patient for forty-five minutes. She likes those patients, the ones who make her think and challenge her abilities, but today, she wants to be done.

In another twenty minutes she's outside waiting, a few minutes early and glad to be out of he clinic. She sits on the bench in the sun, enjoying a few minutes of relaxation. As she closes her eyes, her cell phone rings and she quickly pulls it out of her purse, thinking Richard may be calling to tell her they're on their way. Instead, she's disoriented by a 303 area code, followed by a familiar arrangement of numbers: Colorado. Art. She stares at the phone as it rings, her thumb poised above the answer button. She tenses as she thinks of answering it, then exhales as the rings stop. She shoves it back into her purse and ignores the hums it makes to indicate a voice mail has been left. Looking up, she scans the cars for Richard and Ken.

They arrive at the restaurant half an hour before their reservation, and Ken looks at the wine list while Rosie and Richard view the menu. In fifteen minutes, they're brought to their table near the window, where they can view the setting sun as it descends upon the Pacific. Most of the tables are arranged for the view, and the restaurant is already almost full. Rosie is distracted by the thought of her cell phone, knowing it will read "New Voicemail" when she finally looks at it, and she considers what she might hear when she finally listens to the message. She's not pulled down by these thoughts though, and she concentrates on the present and the reality before her, happily joining in the conversation. Ken talks eloquently about wine, speaking of vintages and bouquets romantically with articulate and thoughtful language. The wine arrives and she swirls it dutifully, smiling at her friends who offer a sophisticated evaluation. In the ensuing pause, they all turn to look at the sunset. It's glorious. The sun disappears behind a cloud and the sky is bathed in magnificent color. It reappears as a red globe, sinking slowly into the sea as everyone, including the wait staff, turns to watch. The water seems calmed by the shift from day to dusk to nightfall. The three of them toast her birthday.

They order succulent meals. The laughter and warmth are absent of cardboard, paper, and ribbon but present an absolutely perfect gift. It's everything she's wished for. She thinks momentarily of Colorado snow, and she shudders. Her life, indeed, is today a celebration. As they leave, Richard puts his arm around her and kisses her on the cheek. "Happy Birthday, honey! I'm glad you're back."

"Me, too," she smiles. "And thanks for dinner!" He squeezes her shoulder tighter.

As they drive back home she thinks of her journey back to the Bay. She'd left Colorado on a Friday, driving into the setting sun. She drove straight through, stopping for gas and at a rest stop to shut her eyes for an hour. Staying at a hotel, alone, was too solitary a prospect, so she'd pushed through and arrived in San Francisco while a foggy rain fell. She'd driven through Pacific Heights, unable to locate their home, and frantically called Richard. He'd donned yellow rain gear and waited for her outside, helping her park, showing her in, and finding her tissue when she sat sobbing on the couch, choking out, "I . . . screwed . . . up." Ken had fixed a Manhattan while Richard patted her back and held out more tissue.

Ken is a successful architect, and he and Richard agreed to rent Rosie the mother-in-law apartment he'd designed as part of his house.

The situation works well. Days go by when they don't see each other, but they still frequently share meals and funny stories about their days. Richard works as a hospice administrator in the old Presidio Army base. The building provides a peaceful last residence for up to ten patients, and he and his staff work diligently to maintain a serene environment, attentive to last wishes of clients and their families. They spend down time planting flowers in the small yard or pulling weeds.

When Rosie first arrived back in the city, she'd volunteered at the hospice. She spent afternoons or mornings sitting with patients who wanted company, or voiced a fear of death and dying alone. She'd hold their hands or lay a hand on their arm, and watched as the lines on their faces smoothed with comfort. She pulled old thoughts out of her mind, sifting through mistakes that embarrassed her, as she pulled weeds from the garden, and looking at the healthy plants brought her an evenness and confidence she hadn't felt in months. Since she had to wait for forwarded mail, her letter declaring she had passed the boards arrived three days after Richard's. The three days were long, but the relief matched that length in joy. Her confidence grew. She felt blissfully at home.

"Did you remember the lamp today?" Ken asks her from the front seat.

"Sorry?" She leans forward in the car.

"You know, for your . . . what do you call them? Girl exams?"

She laughs. "Well woman exam." Ken refers to her first pap smear she'd had to perform, when she prepared speculum, brush, slide, and gloves, but forgotten to move the lamp in from the other room. The moment still makes her blush, even though her patient had been extremely understanding. She'd had the speculum already positioned before she realized she could see absolutely nothing. "Yes, I did. Thanks for asking."

"I'm glad I don't have to do those." Richard states. "That's really not needed at the hospice." Ken gives him a look which Rosie can't see, but she giggles anyway.

"Yeah, I finally got one done smoothly, almost like I knew what I was doing." They laugh. "There's just so much to know, you know? Even with school and clinicals, I still feel like I have SO MUCH to learn. And I hate it that I sometimes just don't know. I feel like I have to go ask the doctor everything."

"You have to know what you don't know," Ken states and Richard agrees. "If I were your patient, I'd rather have you tell me you weren't sure than have you randomly make something up."

"I guess. I just need to be better at finding the answers."

Ken describes his fledgling years as an architect, explaining the projects he'd done, and how much support he'd needed from the senior partners at the firm. "In some ways," he says thoughtfully, "I might have been better then. The conscientiousness made me pay attention in a way I don't necessarily do now."

"You're talking about complacency?" Richard asks.

"No, not really complacency. At least, I don't want to admit it might be complacency!" He laughs and then pauses. "I think something more like Zen. Something like that rapture you get when something is new. When you do something for the first time, whether you do it perfectly or not, you don't forget it, simply because the details of it are so clear in your mind's eye." He catches her eye in the rear view mirror. She nods slowly. The engine hums and the sound of the tires passing smoothly over asphalt is soothingly monotonous. They drift off into their own thoughts.

The position in internal medicine opened up two weeks after she arrived, and she applied, knowing there would be competition. The pay was low, compared with other clinics, but when the job was offered, she took it. Now she climbs quickly up the learning curve, managing hypertension to depression, completing physicals and squinting at skin lesions. She's embarrassed every time she has to ask for help, but reminds herself that asking isn't for her, it's for her patients. She learns quickly, and before long, begins to grow comfortable with the medications she prescribes and the advice and teaching she gives to patients. Counseling of some form, whether nutritional guidance or discussing depression and anxiety, is a large part of her role as a nurse practitioner. The first time her patient with high cholesterol comes back for a repeat draw after diet changes and exercise, she's elated when she can call and tell him the results are normal, and to "keep up the good work!"

In June, she joins Richard and Ken on a Saturday morning walk along the bay. They bring Sammy, their Jack Russell terrier to this spot every week. Sammy romps with joy along the sand, barking at the gulls, digging little holes and sniffing, and looking back at them with her mouth open as if grinning "Thank you!" They stroll slowly, meandering along the sand, having a conversation which flows like a slow moving river.

"I like the view here." Richard states, and Rosie admires the Golden Gate Bridge, the deep orange contrasting dramatically with the blue Bay. She smiles and nods while Richard lightly slaps her arm. "What?" she asks, not registering that he's looking in the opposite direction. She sees him gesture toward the wind surfers who have arrived and are setting up their equipment. They're clad in wetsuits, some unzipped to the waist, and the muscles in their arms bulge as they maneuver to the water. Rosie laughs. "Oh, THAT view!"

She looks twice at a man who turns back to say something to his friend. She's sure he's familiar, and searches her memory for where she's seen his face. A patient? No, she's sure she'd remember a patient like him. It's definitely a memory from San Francisco. In a flash, she knows, picturing the café and the textbook Dr. Davids had given her, the moment his son had winked at her, and her glass of water into which she'd hidden her smile.

"Trey?" She half shouts the question into the breeze. He looks up; they're only about thirty feet away, now. She's sure it's him. "Trey!" He smiles in recognition and she jogs over.

When she reaches him, she's suddenly aware of how dense the sand is and she's out of breath. She wants to hug him, but stops herself, knowing they've only met once before. The sensation of knowing him, but feeling like a stranger is vertiginous. He rearranges his load and reaches a hand toward her, which she gratefully grasps. Immediately, she's righted, sensing both his the strength and the solid reassuring ground beneath her. She feels the endurance of her pounding heart. She raises a hand to shield the sun as she looks up at him.

"It's good to see you!" she says with sincerity.

"Rosie! Hey! I thought you were in Colorado?"

"Yeah," she takes a breath. "That didn't work out so well."
Sammy bounces over to them as Richard and Ken approach.

"Hey pup!" Trey looks down.

"These are my friends, Richard and Ken. And Sammy."

"Good to meet you." They shake hands and look toward the
water.

"Looks like it will be a great day out there!" Ken tells him.

"I think so. Do you windsurf?"

"I tried it once, but it was too hard! And, at the time, I didn't
have the time to commit to learning it." Ken looks at Sammy, who has
her head cocked and ears up, eager for her next sprint.

"You should try it again. It's addictive." Sammy jumps from her
sitting position to chase a gull and Richard and Ken excuse themselves to
follow her. Trey looks at Rosie.

"So what happened to Colorado?"

"It just never clicked for me. I was there for almost six months
and it never felt like home."

Trey nods with understanding. "I felt like that once. I had to come back to the Bay." He looks across it nostalgically, then turns to her with a smile. "Well, welcome back!"

"Thanks. How's your Dad?"

"Good. The same. Stubborn!" He looks at the other windsurfers and waves to a friend, who looks as if he's prepared to paddle out.

"I better catch up with them. It's good to see you!" He starts to walk down the sand. She feels as if thrown down from a height of excitement as she stands in the sand, watching him. She begins to rise as he stops and turns back to her.

"Hey, do you want to get coffee later?"

She smiles and carefully attempts to sound casual, "Sure, that would be great!"

He jogs back to her as she steps forward. "I don't have a pen or anything . . .. Let's see, can we meet in Berkeley? Telegraph?"

Rosie has reached into her jean pocket and retrieves her phone. "That's sounds great! I can call you, if you want." He steps closer to her to watch her enter his number. She can feel the hairs on her arm brush his.

She runs to where Richard and Ken have caught up with Sammy, oblivious to the effort that running in sand entails.

"Did you get a date with one on the hot windsurfers?" Richard asks her. She nods quickly.

"Not TOO jealous there, honey."

"Never." Richard pats him. Rosie looks around. It really is a gorgeous day.

The BART rising out from under the Bay is always like coming to another country, for Rosie. She leaves the station and walks to Telegraph Ave, finding the coffee shop Trey had described. she sees him at a table, and waves as he gets up to meet her. He looks good in khaki shorts and a polo shirt. His strides over to her are relaxed yet deliberate.

"Thanks for coming to this side of the Bay. I needed time to shower up."

"No problem. I like excuses to come over here."

He nods and looks at the board. "Do you want something?" She orders a latte and before she can get her money out, he's paid for it. They move to a table in the sun. She asks about his morning, his physical therapy practice, and his family; he asks about her current position, her living arrangement with Richard and Ken, and her journey to and from Colorado. She's finally able to laugh about the job she had there, and Amelia's condescending and denigrating treatment of her. Now that she's finally working as a nurse practitioner, she appreciates the discrepancy between RN and NP, and enjoys her role. They joke about snowboarding, and she shakes her head recalling the physical pain of it that lasted a full week.

"Why did you go out there in the first place?" Trey asks her. He leans in to talk to her, and the way he listens makes her feel heard; she articulates with ease and answers his questions more thoroughly than she's been able to give answers to herself. His eyes are a rich brown, and she senses herself falling into them. But to this question she balks, sips her latte, and looks away. "I had a friend who lived out there—lives out there. He talked me into moving."

"Oh." Trey leans back and she shakes her head quickly, wanting to retrieve the intimacy that he has backed away from.

"He's a friend from Peace Corps. I felt like . . ." she looks at her hands, searching for the right explanation. "After graduate school, I thought I had to move on, in a literal sense, and, for some reason, I didn't think I could do it here. But I didn't know where to go, and, my friend," she sighs. "Peace Corps becomes like family." Trey nods. "I think I was scared to go and afraid to stay here, and so I went where I felt like I'd have family."

Trey intently nods, appearing to digest what she's said. "Patient care is scary, there's no doubt. Especially if you care about your patients. But if it's what you want to do, you just have to start doing it."

"How long have you been a PT?"

"Going on fifteen years. Well, thirteen, I guess. I took a sabbatical in there." He smiles.

"A sabbatical?"

He clears his throat. "I was married for a few years. Five years, total." He sheepishly looks at her and his reticence is odd. It's a part of him that doesn't mesh with his otherwise confident and outgoing personality. "She was career focused, and got a position which made us move to New York."

"The city?"

"Yup. It was a good set up. We had a great apartment and she was making a lot of money. I had trouble finding a job. I finally got something doing workman's comp. Yeah." He points to the disgusted face she's made. "But it just didn't work for me. I missed my family. I missed the Bay Area."

"New York City is fun—it can be great. But it's not here."

"Exactly. So, we talked, we argued, we did some couples counseling. She stayed and here I am." Rosie can't think how to respond. The space between them rings with silence. "It taught me a lot," he says softly, slowly. "We met when I was in graduate school, and I didn't know who I was at the time. That lack of self-awareness put me in a position that I couldn't see who she was, either. When I found the answers to both of those questions, when *we* found out, going our separate ways seemed obvious."

"That makes sense. I think I found that out in Denver. You have to know who you are and where home is. If you aren't home, . . ."

"Nothing works." He completes her sentence and she smiles.

They walk back to the BART together, and he describes the shops and restaurants they pass. They talk about food, and she tells him about her Italian heritage, and the meatballs and sauce her grandmother made.

"Did she give you the recipe?"

"Oh no. Just, a little bit of this, a little bit of that. She evaded our direct questions and keep it mysterious."

"So you couldn't reproduce them?"

"Well, I think I'm close." She looks at him as they reach the entrance to the BART.

"Maybe you could make them for me sometime? I'm a pretty good food critic. I'll give you my honest opinion!" He holds the door open for her as she laughs at his joke.

"I'd like that. But you'll have to buy me dinner, in exchange." She leans in toward him and he smiles.

"Agreed."

When she gets home, Richard is unloading groceries. She grabs a few bags to help him.

"Thanks!" He looks at her. "You look nice. How was coffee?"

"Excellent!"

"You're glowing. Or are you blushing? Who is this guy, anyway?"

"I didn't tell you?" She begins to explains as he sorts groceries and she sits at the bar watching him, telling him about how they first met, the conversation in Berkeley, and the pictures of him as a toddler. "I feel like I know him already, like I just met him but I *really* know him. And I feel I've always known him."

"Hm. Like fate."

"Yeah." She strings out the word as Richard rolls his eyes upward. He rips open a bag of miniature carrots and pops one into his mouth, then extends the bag toward her.

"Carrot?"

She dreams that night of the sea. It's an expanse of water that resembles everywhere she's ever been—Africa, Florida, Maine, California, and she's looking at the waves and froth one moment. In the next she's under the water, swaying with seagrass and coral, watching colorful fish glide by and somehow breathing underwater unaided. She's weightless, serene, timeless, and strong. The surface and the floor of the sea are one in her vision; she is at once everywhere. Moving but still. Separate but whole. Looking up, the surface of the water has an alive, wonderous quality, like living glass. The sun comes in through her window in the morning and she opens her eyes smiling.

At work on a Wednesday she walks into an exam room to see a thin woman looking at her expectantly, possibly with anger. Immediately, Rosie is on guard, prepared to dislike her and quickly wrap up a visit that this woman probably didn't want to come to. Rosie asks her why she's come in and she describes her problem—heartburn, to the extent she feels things get stuck in her throat. Rosie begins to talk about diet changes, smoking habits, which she can smell on her clothes, and over-the-counter remedies. Her patient gets angry, interrupting her to tell her that the doctor in the same office already told her "all this stuff" six months ago. Rosie stops, looks at her, and realizes it's fear, not anger, emitting from her. She tries to leaf through the chart, but can't hold it on her lap to do so, so she stands and opens it on the exam table. "When were you here?" "January." She finds the progress note and compares the woman's weight on that visit and the one today. She's lost twenty-five pounds. She reads the note, seeing the suggestions the doctor made, which, as the patient stated, are similar to her own. At the bottom of the page, she sees that blood work was ordered and she turns to the lab section. The room is quiet. The complete blood count reveals anemia. The doctor had signed off on the labs with an "OK" and his initials.

"Wait here." She says to the patient, and turns to walk out. She stops, turns back. "Let me just take a quick look at you." She checks lymph nodes, listens to her lungs and heart, and gently palpates her abdomen. Nothing is abnormal, but the examination gives her time to think.

"Okay." She sits down and looks at her. "I'm concerned about your symptoms and your weight loss. Your blood work was . . ." she doesn't know what to say so she starts again. "I think you need to see a gastroenterologist, and I'm going to go call his office to see when they can get you in."

"The sooner the better." She tells her. She gets up. When her hand is on the door, she turns to her. "Actually, why don't you come with me while I call."

The patient sits nervously in her office while she calls the gastroenterologist's office. She asks to speak to the nurse.

"I have a patient here with a six month history of dysphagia, documented 25 pound weight loss, and a low hematocrit." She reads off the numbers and tries not to react when the nurse says esophageal cancer. Rosie affirms this concern glances up at the patient.

"They can get you in Friday, is that okay?" She nods.

After she hangs up, she gets up and shakes her hand. "Thanks, doc." Rosie starts to explain she's not a doctor, and describes her position and role. The woman appears unfazed. "Well, you're a doctor to me." Rosie watches her walk down the hall to leave, her clothes sagging, and hopes she's wrong about the diagnosis.

She goes home and knocks on Richard and Ken's door, opening it when she hears Richard yell, "Come in!" He's sitting by the window when she enters and she joins him in an adjacent chair.

"How was your day?" he asks her.

"Well, I may have a client for you." She shakes her head. "How was yours?"

"We had a death. It was a hard one." Rosie already knows that some of the passings are peaceful and timely, while others seem unfair, or difficult.

"What happened?"

"She was 26. A beautiful girl who was diagnosed with ovarian cancer six months ago. She was from Marin County. Can you believe they chose us over Marin?" Rosie smiles, knowing Richard is using humor to hide his sorrow. His eyes are red and swollen. "She just had everything going for her. She was engaged when she found out, and the guy, to his credit, stuck by her until the end. The family is just in pieces and we're doing our best to help them out."

"I'm sorry, Richard. That's hard."

"Well, I guess it's part of the business, hunh?" He smiles and she covers his hand with hers. "What about your patient?" he asks.

"Uh. I saw this woman who probably has esophageal cancer. The thing is, she was seen six months ago, and the doctor didn't follow up on an abnormal CBC."

"That sucks. Although, you know, even if he did, there's not a hell of a lot you can do for that one."

"You're right. At least I got her in right away to see GI."

They stare at the view, feeling subdued and glad for each other's company. The days are longer, but the fog dims the light and softens the angles of the structures upon which they gaze. They talk quietly about small things, letting a peaceful silence fill the gaps between their words. Ken comes home to break the spell and interrupt the mourning. Richard rises to give him a hug to welcome him home.

At eight o'clock Trey's phone number flashes on Rosie's phone, and she eagerly answers, ignoring her own rules about waiting for the third ring after a first date. The light hearted, flirtatious conversation is welcome after her stressful day and solemn evening. They plan to have dinner on Saturday. He tells her he will take her to a great Vietnamese place, and she agrees. When they hang up, she's surprised an hour has gone by. The phone feels hot in her hand, and she puts it down. Her cell phone still has one unheard message. In the quiet of her apartment, she assesses how she feels, and, after a moment, decides she's ready.

Art's message is short, a little choppy, but absent of moroseness. She notices that he sounds either superficial or uncomfortable. Life is so different and so much better for her now, and calling him means returning to a dark, bad dream. Still, after ten years, and a strong connection, she doesn't want to let the friendship die. Time, she thinks, needing more of it to wash her wounds. Not wanting to call him, she decides to write an e-mail: short, somewhat aloof, appreciative of his efforts, and open. She leaves out the details of her life, but does tell him how she feels that she's come home. Reading and re-reading it, she blinks hard and clicks on the send icon. The room is quiet as she sits for a few minutes looking at the screen, as if watching the message circle and float away over the Sierras, across the dessert, past the continental divide, and finally descend into Denver.

Two weeks go by and she watches her patient walk in slowly with her husband. Rosie's already spoken to the gastroenterologist, and the tissue biopsy confirmed esophageal cancer. Now the patient has seen the oncologist, the surgeon, and the gastroenterologist again. She talks to the doctor who supervises her about the diagnosis and prognosis, letting him look at the chart and find the labs that were checked off and filed. When he sees them, he stops. "How did these get filed?" he asks, and Rosie doesn't answer. His question is almost accusatory, and Rosie purposely doesn't respond. She's puzzled that he doesn't collapse with guilt or at least demonstrate some degree of personal responsibility. Still, he comes in with her to the exam room, and they talk realistically to the patient about her options and her future. The doctor exits, and Rosie spends more time answering questions and stressing quality of life to the patient. She explains pain can and should be managed. She also stressing the importance of stool softeners once narcotic pain medications are given. The patient begins to cry. Her husband blinks back tears and reaches for his wife's hand. Rosie hands them tissues, and respectfully looks away. As they leave she wants to be able to do more, but she's glad to have been able to do what she has.

"Please call us if there's anything you need, anything we can do." They nod. The woman at the front desk reiterates this, and they watch quietly as the door closes behind them. The woman at the front desk looks down and states, almost inaudibly, "That should have been caught six months ago." Rosie nods without looking at her.

On July 4th, Rosie meets Trey to watch the fireworks over the Bay. On separate occasions, they've had coffee, lunch, and dinner, and the dates are beginning to lengthen past nightfall. They talk almost every night, and his wit brings light into her days. She tries to reciprocate by listening to the issues he faces at work; challenges with front office staff's quitting, or new techniques he's learned and is trying to master. While listening to him she learns how intelligent he is, and how very sensitive. In subtle ways, he reminds her of his father. At first this reminder was uncomfortable and a little creepy, but it has shifted to endearing. She brings a picnic to the open field and Ken supplies her with a bottle of wine he deems appropriate. They sit close together as the sky begins to fill with explosive color, and as the evening begins to chill he puts his arm around her. She turns to him as white sparkles whistle and twist down from the sky and they kiss. After three weeks of dating, the warm, physical contact is a relief and she can't help but smile as their lips part then meet again. He pulls away from her; "What?"

"It took you long enough." His laughter mingles with the popping noises above them, and the oohs and aahs of surrounding onlookers, craning their necks to look at the sky. She closes her eyes to kiss him again.

Rosie feels herself falling in love. She talks to her mother on the phone and doesn't mind when she hears her yell to her father "John! Rosie has a boyfriend!" She can picture her mother cover the mouthpiece as she shouts across the house. Although she can't hear her father's reply, it's easy for her to imagine what he's said. Instead of being annoyed, she laughs, and tells her mother about Trey, assuring her that he's a gentleman when she asks.

Her days at work go by and get easier. As her confidence grows, she's reminded of Ken's recollection of being a young architect. Every time Rosie enters an exam room, she pauses to remind herself the patient she is about to see is not the patient she's seen before. She holds on to the door handle and clicks it open to walk into the present, listening to the patient's specific complaint. Her office visits are slightly longer than those of the physicians with whom she works, but she's glad to spend the extra time getting to know her patients and teaching them how to be healthy. There are patients who come seeking narcotics, and there are others who return frequently, wanting Rosie to find some strange disease from which they suffer. These visits are tedious, littered with vague complaints or long lists of symptoms detailed in five minute increments throughout the day. She welcomes it when they switch care to one of the two physicians in the office. Twice a month she and the two doctors meet to review difficult cases and exchange ideas. As the months go by, Rosie feels she can contribute to the conversation, rather than simply present her cases. The knowledge and experience fill her with pride.

The Wednesday after July 4th she has dinner with Ken and Richard. They've fallen into a routine of eating together on this day, and Rosie makes a salad and buys a baguette to accompany the chicken Ken roasts.

"So how's it going with your man?" Richard winks at Rosie.

"Good," she smiles. "Great."

"How were the fireworks? Explosive?"

She laughs. "Yeah."

"How was the wine?"

"Really good. Was that the vineyard that you mentioned?"

"Uh hunh. In Sonoma. We're going up this weekend if you want me to pick you up some bottles."

"Sure, that would be great." She adds: "This chicken is fantastic."

"Thanks."

"I have an idea," Richard interjects. "Why don't you and Trey come with us."

"To Sonoma?"

"Sure. We could do some wine tasting. With the pro." He gestures toward Ken.

"I guess." She thinks about it. "Yeah. I'll ask Trey. That could be fun. Are you going for the day?"

"We always stay at this place in Sonoma—even when we go to Napa. You know, after tasting, it's a long drive back. Should we reserve two rooms?" His smile is sly as he looks at Rosie. She blushes. "I don't know about that yet. How about we take two cars and go from there."

On Saturday Trey picks her up while Richard and Ken finish putting things in the car. Ken has a special case he uses to transport the bottles of wine, and Trey helps him maneuver it into the trunk of the car. Sammy looks on suspiciously, then leaps in with joy when she realizes she can go. Trey confirms the location of the restaurant where they'll meet for lunch before visiting the vineyards.

It's a beautiful day in Sonoma, one that makes foggy, damp San Francisco seem like a myth. They sit outside to eat lunch so that Sammy can stay with them, loosely leashed between Ken and Richard's chairs with a bowl of water between her feet. Ken unwraps some of the prosciutto from his melon and hands it to her. She looks as though she were on holiday. "Would you like a massage after lunch?" Richard leans over to ask her. She paws at his knee.

They leave already relaxed, focused but unhurried. Ken recites a plan, having already thought of the best places they all will enjoy. Richard checks into the bed and breakfast and they leave Trey's car there. Trey and Rosie share the back seat with Sammy, who sits up eagerly between them. Sammy turns to lick Trey's face when he scratches her ears.

The wine is good, and Rosie and Trey follow Ken's suggestions as they taste it. By the third vineyard, they feel professional; and Trey and Rosie stand at the crowded counter a few feet away from Richard and Ken.

Richard taps Rosie on the shoulder. "We're going to shop around a little in the store," he tells them. "Will you kids be okay by yourselves?"

"I think so," Rosie answers.

"What do you think of this one?" Trey asks her. She swirls. She smells. She takes a sip and lets it rest on her tongue.

"Hmm. Nice bouquet. Complex. Blackberries?"

Trey shrugs and nods.

"Good, what did Ken call it? Maturity?"

"I think he said complete. Or am I confusing it with complex?" They giggle and she leans into his shoulder. "Anyway, I think it's good."

"Me, too." She finishes her glass.

"Come on. Let's take a walk outside." He takes her hand.

They walk along the paths through the vineyard, holding hands, taking their time. Rosie feels the pleasant warmth of the wine humming in her head, coupled with the warmth of the proximity to Trey.

"Beautiful day, hunh?" he says, squinting at the blue sky.

"It is. It's nice to be out of the city. It feels like we're so far away."

"Yeah."

They reach a gazebo and stop. They look at each other and kiss.

"I don't want to leave," she tells him, with her eyes still closed.

"Well, we don't have to."

She opens her eyes and looks at him, puzzled.

"Well, not tonight anyway." Her body floods with excitement yet she's suddenly nervous. She hugs him, melting as his arms wrap around her. He smells good. She's ready for this. "Okay," she tells him. A gentle wind rustles the grapevines and the vines shudder against their trellises. They wrap around the solid support and twist themselves into a

146

comfortable symbiosis, since the trellises, too, lean toward them. Swaying slightly, heavy with fruit, the plants hang on tenaciously. A butterfly moves by, jostled by air currents, riding them up and down like the breath of laughter. The white paint of the gazebo shines in the sun, almost smelling of paint, the coat is so fresh. Sunlight bathes the blue sky and every leaf moves toward it, stretching, pulling, and beautifully alive.

Rosie prepares for the cook-out with care and deliberation. She will meet Trey's mother, and see his father. The gathering already feels uncomfortable, now that she's sleeping with his son. Trey will pick her up in half an hour. She stares at the array of shirts in front of her, her fingernail between her teeth. She hears footsteps above and runs out the door, up the steps, and raps on the door. "Richard!" She shouts. "Fashion advice! STAT!" He opens the door and looks at her with his eyebrows raised. "Ken's the artist," he tells her calmly.

"Hunh?" Ken asks from the couch, where he's reading the paper.

"Rosie needs fashion advice. She's meeting The Mother today."

"Ah," he doesn't look up. "Got any mumus?"

Rosie has had a month of learning. She's learned that Trey keeps his house immaculate, and doesn't like towels to be folded or crumpled onto the rack. When she enters, she takes off her shoes. She knows exactly how long it takes to get from the door of her office to his front door. He has a cat with whom she's befriended, and she knows where the food is kept as well as the treats that maintain her good standing, from the feline's perspective. Trey make the lattes in the morning, and she enjoys watching him move domestically through the kitchen. She knows that her meatballs are still just almost as good as her grandmother's, no matter what she tries. Waking up with Trey is comforting, exciting, and that his hands are strong, tender, and sensuous. The way her body fits into his is electric.

There are other things she continues to learn. Paperwork is cumbersome at work. Patient's don't always follow advice, and she can do very little to change behavior. She discovers some medicines work better and are cheaper than others, and she finds that public advertisement of medicine makes her work more difficult. She also knows that if she inadvertently prescribes a more expensive medicine, the patient will return furious at her. Meanwhile the drug company, which set the invisible price tag upon the pills within the bottle, will continue its business unscathed. She enjoys meetings with drug representatives until she find out how much these half hour slots cost her patient's. From a nurse in the office, she is appalled to learn the physician she works with is having an affair with a nurse in another office, who is also married. She's told that the affair was discovered when a medical assistant opened an exam door to discover the exam table inappropriately in use. At meetings now, she has trouble looking him in the eye. She also learns how to do a referral to hospice, when her patient with esophageal cancer develops complications after surgery, cannot tolerate the chemotherapy, continues to lose weight, and decides to accept comfort measures only. The patient made an appointment with her simply to say good-bye. She had given Rosie a tearful hug, Rosie's own eyes welling up as well, and then thanked her as her husband helped her shuffle out.

Rosie looks in the mirror, Ken beside her, and she twists back and forth to observe what he's chosen for her. He takes her by the shoulders and tells her to relax. She sighs, thanks him with a hug, and walks with him to the door.

When Trey arrives to pick her up, she's confident in the conservative outfit which Ken has approved. She hurries into Trey's car and kisses him. "I missed you," he says and she smiles and tells him "me, too." They hold hands in the car for most of the fifteen minute drive.

Dr. Davids's home is modest, reflecting his personality. His wife, Trey's mother Kate, greets her with a hug.

"You must be Rosie!" she exclaims. Rosie's first impression is that Kate is as outgoing as Dr. Davids is quiet. "I've heard so much about you! Come in!"

Rosie follows her through the living room and into the kitchen. There's a door out of the kitchen onto a small deck, and Dr. Davids hovers over a grill in a grease stained apron, looking much as he does in his lab coat, standing over a patient. In the first moment she sees him though she has trouble recognizing him. He's stooping, which makes him appear shorter, and he also looks thin. "James and Kelly are on their way," Kate explains, referring to Trey's brother and sister-in-law, and Rosie breaks her concerned gaze away from Dr. Davids and smiles at Kate.

"How is she feeling?" Rosie asks, knowing that Kelly is now six months pregnant.

"She's fine, much better than the first trimester!"

"You must be excited."

"That doesn't begin to describe it. My first grandbaby!"

"Hey Dad!" Trey walks out the door to hug his father and Rosie follows him. Dr. Davids' smiles at his son and they embrace. He then turns to Rosie and hugs her.

"Good to see you again."

"Likewise," she says. She stands back and looks at him, noticing his face is thinner. She consciously smiles to avoid demonstrating her concern. "How are you?"

"Good! You?" He turns back to the grill. Trey touches her back and she tenses, not sure how to respond in the presence of his parents.

"Good," she tells him. "I'm going to see if your mom needs any help, okay?" She turns before Trey can kiss her, but looks back in time to see him wink at her.

Kate asks her to transfer the potato salad into a bowl, then chop some vegetables for a salad. Keeping her hands occupied helps her focus and enables her to feel her feet on the ground. She hears Ken's voice in her head, telling her to relax, and she smiles at Trey when he looks at her with an expression that asks, is everything okay in there?

"How's Dr. Davids's practice going?" She asks Kate.

"Jim's? You can call him Jim. Oh, you know. He works too much. It takes its toll on him." She glances toward him. Rosie reads Kate's face carefully before she says, "He looks like he's lost a little weight." She looks into the salad, attempting nonchalance.

"He has. For the first time in years I had to buy him 34 pants."

"But he feels okay, right?"

"Well, he's tired. It seems like he gets tired more easily these days."

"He probably just needs to take that vacation Trey keeps insisting on." Rosie's comment is meant to be humorous, but Kate doesn't laugh, and her silence concerns Rosie. Oh God, she thinks, I screwed up. She hates me now. She looks desperately toward Trey, but his back is to her, and his hand gestures indicate he's engrossed in conversation with his father. Kate eases her fears.

"It's more than that, honey. It's . . ." she looks toward him. "I'm just worried. He's a doctor, you know? They're the worst patients in the world!"

Rosie's not sure how to respond. "Can I set the table for you?" Kate touches her shoulder and leads her to the silverware.

James and Kelly arrive, and they soon arrange themselves around the table. The conversation is relaxed, and James and Trey tease each other like children. James has a slighter build than Trey, and more hair, but their faces look similar, especially when they smile. Rosie is relieved that much of the attention is focused on Kelly and her growing belly which Kate is already smiling at adoringly. They finish with bountiful compliments to Jim and Kate. Trey and James stand up to clear the table, and Jim goes out to clean the grill. Rosie automatically observes Jim's meager intake of food as his plate is carried away.

"Are you working now?" Rosie asks Kelly.

"Uh hunh. I'm in sales, not too far from the University."

"That's near where I work, then."

"Really? Do you practice on the medical campus?"

"Professional building 3." Rosie states with mock formality. Kelly laughs.

"We should have lunch, sometime."

"Definitely! So you're eating okay? How has work been?"

"It was harder a few months ago. Now that my energy level is better and the nausea has improved, it's pretty much business as usual. With more snacks." They laugh. "And bigger lunches."

"Will you take off time, when the baby is born?"

"Definitely, but I'm not sure how much. I might even resign. It's just hard to pay the bills if I do that." Kelly looks out the window with her hand on her belly then turns back. Kate excuses herself to use the bathroom. "What about you, do you think you'll have kids?"

Rosie smiles, blushing. "Well, eventually. Probably. Not in the next nine months, though!"

"He seems to really like you." Kelly tells her.

Rosie leans toward her in a conspiring manner. "Really? Do you think so?" Kate nods, giggling with Rosie. "Well, I really like him to." She begins to feel like a ten year old, so she adds, "he's just so . . . genuine. And sweet. And fun to be with."

"They're both good men. When things didn't work out with—he told you about his ex, right?"

"Yeah."

"Phew. That would have been a foot in the mouth. But when it didn't work out, it was almost a relief."

Rosie feels hopeful. She's had a nagging thought that maybe Trey was still attached to his former wife. "Why's that?"

"She was too into her career. To an extreme. She was the kind of woman who didn't mind stepping on people on her way to the top. And this family is really about family, and caring about other people. It just didn't fit."

"What didn't fit?" Kate steps back into the room, holding a book.

"Sylvia."

"Oh. You can say that again." She looks at Rosie. "Not that we wish her any harm. She just wasn't right for Trey. But speaking of right . . ." she hands the book to Kelly. Rosie sees "names" in the title and watches as Kelly forces a smile and opens it right away. "Thanks," she glances at Rosie. Rosie feels part of the family and doesn't mind when Trey comes back and rests a hand on her shoulder.

As they're getting ready to leave, Jim stops Rosie.

"Rosie," he begins. "Before you go, I want to ask you something." Rosie's afraid of what he might say, thinking it must be in relation to Trey. "I've applied for a grant for the clinic."

"Oh, yeah. I think you were talking about that last summer."

"Right. Well, if I get it, and it's a big if, I can hire on at least one full time nurse practitioner, and possibly a part time physician. Is that something you'd be interested in?"

Rosie feels excited at the possibility of working in the familiar clinic. "Yes, definitely! Do you know when?"

"Probably sometime in the new year. I'll keep you posted."

"Sure. Yes, whatever I can do to help." Jim smiles at her and pats her shoulder. She momentarily wonders what kinds of conversations he had had about her before she and Trey met, and to what degree they've been set up. As she looks over at Trey, who has his arm around his brother, she ceases to care.

"How did you get into HIV care, anyway?" he asks her. They're walking through the redwood forest in late September, comforted by the protective presence of the enormous trees.

"We haven't talked about this?"

"No. At least I don't think so." He takes her hand as the path widens.

"I had a friend who got HIV. It was a long time ago. Well, it feels like a long time ago. When I was in Peace Corps."

"That was . . . early '90s?"

"About that. It was before protease inhibitors."

"Ah. The AIDS era. What was it called then—gay cancer?"

"Yeah." Rosie laughs at the archaic term. Talking to Trey about it is easy, since he's familiar with the terms used in HIV care as well as the ignorance, and its harm, in the beginning years of the epidemic. She doesn't have to stop to explain in detail the minutia of care.

"His name was Octavius. He was gay," she adds this before he can ask or begin to infer that the relationship they had had was romantic. Then she feels oddly embarrassed that the statement seemed necessary. "He was this amazing person. He lived—I mean he was one of those people you meet who don't miss a moment and who truly live their life." She sees Trey nod. "I think, at the time, I was trying to figure out stuff. I didn't know what I wanted to do with my life, who I wanted to be, or even who I was. And Octavius helped me find the way to all those answers."

"Sound like a good friend." Despite her explanation, she detects a small amount of jealousy in Trey's voice. She stops walking and looks at him. "You're kidding. You're jealous?"

"No! What?! I mean, should I be?"

Rosie begins to cry, pulling her hand away from his and surprising herself as much as Trey with her unresolved grief and immediate anger. "He's dead, Trey. There's nothing to be jealous of. He died in October, six years ago. He had this beautiful heart and beautiful soul and he helped me SO much and he's dead." She starts to walk quickly, following the path. A few moments pass before she hears Trey's steps jogging up to her.

"Hey." His voice is even and quiet as he gently takes her arm. She stops and collapses into him, letting go of her anger in one thick breath, as he hugs her. She dries her face with her hand and he brushes her hair back. "I'm sorry. That was a stupid thing to say."

"It was the hardest thing I've had to go through. Watching a friend just disappear. The illness just . . . he just wasted away to nothing."

"And you loved him?" He says this quietly, unassumingly, and the words mingle with the rush of wind high in the trees.

She nods.

Trey sighs, looking up.

"Trey," he looks down to her as she raises her eyes to look at him. "Octavius meant a lot to me. He was a good friend and we shared a really intense time together. But I know I need to let go of him. And, mostly, I have."

"It's all right to hang on to people. It's okay to carry them around inside you. I think it helps you do what you do, as a nurse practitioner. It helps you stay focused."

She smiles at him. "I love you." The words fall out of her automatically, as if she's said them over and over to him, and she has; but not out loud, and not like this, locked in his arms with the open air around them. For a moment, she's afraid.

He touches her face and kisses her. "I love you, too."

They walk to a fallen tree as the forest gives way to grass, leading to a cliff above the ocean, they can now see before them. They sit close. She rests her head on his shoulder for a moment and straightens as he begins to talk.

"I never worked in HIV, although I've had some clients who are positive. I think I didn't want to because I lived so close to it when I was growing up. Well, if you call living in your 20s growing up. Every time I'd talk to my dad, he'd have another story of someone who died. He really cares about his patients, and it affected him. And my mom. It was an intense time. The worst of it was when he stopped talking, as if it weren't happening."

"I guess I'm fortunate that I only had one death to witness. God. Knowing how your dad practices, and how much of his heart he puts into his work, that must have been awful."

"It was. When the new drugs came out, it changed things. And the drugs keep getting better. I'm sorry your friend missed that era. Just barely."

"Yeah, me too. But I've started to wonder if surviving would have been good."

"How do you mean?"

"I mean his quality of life. A lot of people who 'made it' suffered from the side effects of the early drugs and the way we didn't know how to dose them."

"I think I remember that. Crazy high doses of AZT and, what was it, six pills three times a day?"

"Or more."

"So he could have lived, but . . ."

"But he might have ended up with liver damage, or painful peripheral neuropathy, or, like some people, creating all kinds of debt and being unable to pay it."

"To everything there's a season."

"Yeah. I guess."

"And 'Octavius'? No abbreviated nickname?"

Rosie smiles. "No. He'd say something like, if my mother wanted me to be called something else, she wouldn't have named me 'Octavius'."

"That's the beauty of a name like 'Trey'."

The expanse of the ocean reassures Rosie once again, and she feels her presence on the log next to Trey as if there were nowhere else for her to be. She tells him how she honors Octavius's death every year, in October, on the anniversary of when his ashes were scattered in the sea. Trey listens, and he's quiet for a moment when she finishes.

"That's odd."

"What?" Rosie's defenses rise.

"No, don't get me wrong. It's just that, there's an irony there."

"How do you mean?"

"Well, the first thing you said about him is that he 'lived.' 'More so that most people,' is how you described it, right?"

"Yeah, he really did."

"So why do you spend so much time honoring his death? Wouldn't it be more appropriate to think about and honor his life? And to really live your own?"

Rosie thinks about the time she spent in Colorado, feeling half awake and unhappy, and how much time she wasted, even though it was only a handful of months. She thinks about what Octavius would have done with six months, and wonders if he would have chastised her for wasting a single moment. Her idolatry comes down, down and she raises her own identity to recognize her worth. The moments of her life can be celebrated. Trey has held up a mirror and she has seen herself, the mistakes she has made because she chose to dwell on death rather than life. She begins to understand.

"Hm." Trey's utterance brings her out of her thoughts.

"What?"

"I was just thinking about my dad. Those early days of AIDS, when he was stressed and overworked, and other times when he worked too hard, he always gained weight."

"Yeah?"

"And now, he's losing weight. He says he's working hard when I ask him about it, but that's not usually what happens."

"He did look thinner. And your mom seemed concerned."

"Oh, yeah." He looks at her. "We've talked about it a lot. It's just hard to convince him to go see his primary care provider."

"I guess all you can do is keep working on it. Make the suggestion, you know, then let him do the rest."

"I guess you're right. I just hope it's nothing."

"Me, too." Rosie curls her arm through his. She struggles not to think clinically, to put aside all she's learned and look out at the ocean. She must allow Jim Davids to have an innocent, meaningless loss of weight. But the word she doesn't want to speak rings back and forth in her mind. Fatigue and weight loss. Red flags flying through the corridors of her mind. Cancer.

In the middle of October, on a Saturday morning, Rosie sits looking at her phone, deciding. Trey is windsurfing with his friends, and he will be back for lunch in a few hours. She tucks her legs under her and clears her throat. Her mouth feels dry. She walks to the kitchette to pour a glass of water. She stops. She returns to her seat on the couch. Plunging, she scrolls quickly through her addresses and presses 'send.' Her heart beats faster and she hears the phone ring on the other end, and she untangles her legs to put her feet on the floor and breathe. She looks out the window.

"Hello?"

"Hi, Art. It's Rosie."

"Rosie! Now I can take you off my list of people least likely to call."

"Funny." But she feels some relief.

"How are you?"

The conversation oddly continues as if there had been no affair, as if the road of their friendship were a vehicle easing down an even downhill grade. They talk about the weather, their jobs, his house, Jenny's career, and how well his leg has healed. She eases back into banter, but with some reserve, knowing where they've been forbids flirtation.

"Rosie. I'm sorry I didn't see you when you left."

"Me, too. I just had to get out of there after . . .."

"Yeah. Well, Jenny just got home." She's glad he's changed the subject; he's skillfully dodged the obstacle of directly addressing their indiscretion.

"Okay. Well, I'm glad I got you."

"Same here. Take care of yourself out there."

"Art," she stops him from hanging up. "One more thing. Do you remember when Octavius' birthday was? It was June but I can't remember the date."

"The 28th. I remember because it's a week after my father's."

"Thanks."

They hang up and the conversation is abandoned rather than finished. The words she had meant to share linger in her mind and her heart, stewing. The conversation was easy, but superficial; several steps away from the intimacy they had once shared in talking to one another about the obstacles and accomplishments of their lives. Her brow remains furrowed, her shoulders tensed. Once again she leans on time to define what will occur to bring them close again as friends or to widen the rift between them. She turns her attention to lunch, knowing that Trey will be hungry when he arrives.

Two days later it's the anniversary of Octavius's death. She pauses in her day, but continues working, convinced that honoring her friend means living her own life. The true date she should think of him is in June.

Rosie continues working in internal medicine, spending her down time daydreaming about returning to Dr. Davids's clinic and distracted by her concern for his health.

A physician she works with, the senior partner, knocks on her open office door and enters with a chart. She looks up from her desk and smiles. He's a thorough doctor, and his work is serious and intense. Despite the meetings and the months they've worked together, he continues to slightly intimidate Rosie.

"Do you remember a Ms. Regina Brown?"

"Not really. Did I see her?"

"About a month ago." He hands her the chart and she looks at her note. She sees her diagnosis of laryngitis and her instruction to take ibuprofen, and to return if the symptoms got worse. "Is she back?"

"She's seeing the ENT. Turns out she has throat cancer."

"Oh my God." She doesn't know what else to say.

"It doesn't look like this loss of voice followed the course of a viral illness. You probably should have asked about a smoking history." Rosie's face turns red as she realizes her error, and she feels dreadful talons of guilt, knowing the significance of her oversight.

She flips through the chart. "I didn't think she was smoking."

"She wasn't. She quit ten years ago."

She hands the chart back after noting the phone number. "I'm so sorry. I'll call her. How do you think she'll do?"

"It's hard to say. We'll have to wait for the ENT report once the tissue is examined. Don't beat yourself up on this, Rosie. Not everyone with a sore throat needs a CT, but anyone with this kind of presentation should make you suspicious." He pauses. "You're at a juncture in your practice now. You know a great deal, and you've developed some confidence, which is good as well as appropriate. But you have a challenge because there are also several things you don't know, simply because you lack experience. You'll get that, don't worry." His smile brings her reassurance. "Just be careful during this period of your professional development. Slow things down if you have to. Cross your T's, dot your i's. Just keep your eyes open." She nods and he turns to walk out. Rosie dials the number. She will apologize, somehow. She knows the best she can do is remember, learn, and not repeat this mistake.

Later in the afternoon she finds the physician and tells him she's spoken to the patient, who appreciates her call but hangs up quickly. She's about to leave his office, then decides to ask his advice.

"I have a friend I wanted to run by you."

"Okay."

"He's about sixty, in decent health, as far as I know. But I'm concerned about him because he's lost a lot of weight and he's complaining of increasing fatigue."

"Any focal symptoms?"

"As far as I know he hasn't complained of anything else bothering him." She tries to remember if Trey or Kate mentioned anything; pain or other complaints Jim has had, but she can't recall anything.

"Is he jaundiced?" Rosie realizes he might have looked slightly yellow when she saw him at dinner a few weeks earlier. The dim lights at that time make her unsure.

"I don't think so."

"It sounds suspicious for cancer, as you know, but fatigue and weight loss aren't diagnostic."

Rosie nods. "And if he's jaundiced, liver cancer?"

"With fatigue, weight loss, and asymptomatic jaundice, your differential is pancreatic cancer." She waits for other possibilities, but he stops there. She feels his compassion as he waits for this information to sink in. "Sorry. You know how aggressively that disease behaves. What kind of insurance does this friend have? I'd be happy to take a look at . . ." He lets the sentence trail off.

"Him." She finishes his sentence. "I don't know. I'll have to look into that. Thanks."

Rosie tells Trey to convince his father subtly to get checked by his physician, and has difficultly avoiding an explanation. Trey becomes annoyed, and she lets the topic go. They travel to Florida for Thanksgiving and he meets her parents, aunts, uncles, cousins, and first cousins once removed. The celebration is wonderful. Rosie introduces Trey, bringing him into the happiness of her family as he enveloped her in the loving nature of his. She's glad to be at home for a long weekend and they stay at her parents home two of the nights, then at a hotel the night before they leave where they reunite lustfully after Rosie's refusal of intimacy in the home and bedroom of her childhood. Trey tells her he barely survives her mother's questioning, but she knows he exaggerates the truth. She reminds him of how she walked in to the kitchen to find them deep in conversation as her mother served him coffee and cake. It had made her smile, reminding her of her grandmother's words, the way to a man's heart is through his stomach.

On the first weekend of December, Rosie helps Kate with a baby shower for Kelly. She anxiously waits for Kelly to open her gift, and is happy when Kelly exclaims she had hoped for the baby sling Rosie purchased. They have lunch together the following week, and talk about layettes and colic in a surprisingly non-banal manner.

The baby girl is born on December 17th. Lila Katherine is seven pounds, three ounces, and 18 inches long. Rosie joins Trey on a visit to the hospital.

They arrive at Kelly's room to find Jim and Kate already there. The lights are dim, and Kelly explains she thinks the fluorescent lighting is too much for her little girl, who is cradled in Kate's arms. Rosie gives Kelly a hug and congratulates her, then goes to stand next to Kate. Trey also hugs his sister-in-law and she and James thank him for the flowers he brought and set by the window. James looks proud, but tired as he leans back in an armchair in the corner.

"Would you like to hold her?" Kate asks. Rosie washes her hands, then takes Lila, and rests her up against her shoulder. The baby molds herself instinctively like living clay and weighs little more than the blankets in which she's wrapped. Rosie looks at Trey, and they exchange a meaningful smile.

They stay for about an hour, then start to leave with Jim and Kate. Lila has begun to stir, and is handed back to her mother with her tiny eyes beginning to open.

"Come on, mom, can I just get one look at my baby granddaughter in the light?" Kelly laughs at Kate's question and agrees. Jim flicks on the lights and they all admire the little face. Rosie looks away from her face and glances at Jim as he comments on Lila. Her glance lengthens. She's overcome with emotion that transitions from joy over the presence of Lila to concern.

She looks at Jim's skin. She hasn't really seen him in full light since Labor Day. Even Jim's eyes have a yellow cast. In the fluorescent light his skin is certainly yellow. She tries to blink it away, to close her eyes and have a miracle change it to a normal hue. She looks again and immediately thinks, jaundice. She feels the gravity of the illness within herself, and she touches Trey. He's looking at Lila, and turns distractedly to Rosie. Seeing her expression, his face changes and without words he follows her tacit instruction to look at his father. He looks back at her. "I need to talk to your dad," she whispers.

They leave. "Can I talk to you for a few minutes?" she says to Jim. They step into the waiting room.

"Everything okay?" He misreads her look and reacts defensively when she tells him he doesn't look well.

"Yes, I'm aware of that." His words sound truncated, as if he wishes the conversation would quickly. "My wife, my sons, and now you—"

"Jim," she stands straighter and states, assertively, "You've lost at least, I don't know, twenty pounds, and you appear jaundiced. You look as though you haven't slept in a week but I know for a fact you're sleeping twelve hours a night. You're not eating. You owe it to your family to find out why this is happening, to do something about it."

She doesn't expect his silence as a reply, and looks at him while he stares at the floor behind her. "Thanks, Rosie." He starts to move away and she grabs his arm. He looks at her hand, surprised, and then at her. He's wearing short sleeves, and his skin suddenly looks dramatically yellow against the back of her hand. He looks beat. Completely defeated and spent. Her heart melts to him, and she tells him, less forcefully and with care, "Look, if it's not cancer, then that's great. But if it is, there might be something you can do about it. Or there might be things you'll want to do, before," she breathes, "before you're unable to. You don't have a lot of control—no one does—but take control of what you can. Dr. Davids, Jim, you know this. In fact, I think you taught me this." Trey and Kate are talking with James down the hall. "They're so worried. So am I." Jim looks at her.

"You know, we're here to celebrate. It's my first grandchild." His anger is full of sorrow.

"And you want all the time you have with her. You want to own that time and make it count."

"I guess it wouldn't hurt to just run some blood work." He looks down again and says, almost inaudibly but this time with sincerity, "thanks, Rosie." He walks back to his wife and puts an arm around her. Rosie follows, slowly, and Trey meets her halfway.

"How'd that go?" His question is anxious.

"Okay. Keep working on him, okay?"

"Thanks. I will. We will."

Rosie takes more time with patients at work. She asks them questions about their current health, and what their health has been like in the past. She inquires about smoking, alcohol use, and the use of recreational drugs. "Any other drugs?" If her voice and demeanor do not change the patients will answer as if she's asked about the weather. When she places her stethoscope on their chest or their back, she listens. She thinks, and she discusses options, inviting them always to return or call if something seems unclear.

On New Year's Eve Trey and Rosie stay with Lila for an hour and a half while her parents go out for a glass of champagne. They go only a few blocks away, promising to return quickly. It's early in the evening, and their getting dressed and leaving the house call for a good deal of coaxing and reassurance from Rosie and Trey. They convince Kelly and James they need a little time for just the two of them, and confidently close the door as they leave. When they've departed, the count down begins. They pass Lila back and forth for a long twenty minutes before she falls asleep.

"She's beautiful," Rosie states, looking at the sleeping face.

"Yeah. Good thing she didn't get my brother's looks!"

"Should I put her down?"

"I wouldn't. We're on a roll." They turn on the TV and listen with the volume turned low. Rosie rocks in the chair.

"It's too bad Kelly can't quit her job."

"Yeah. It sort of sounds like she wants to."

"Well, that, and I think it's good for a mother to raise their kids."

Rosie stops rocking for a moment, then starts again. "What do you mean?"

"My mom stayed home with us, and it was the right thing to do."

"There are a lot of right ways to raise children, Trey. It doesn't mean a woman has to give up her career."

The fact that she's hit a nerve becomes obvious when Trey doesn't respond right away. A tense minutes go by before he finally replies. "You really think your career is more important than bringing up your children?"

"First of all, I don't have children, so you can't accuse me of abusing beings who don't exist. Second, I never said it was more important, but I do think it's almost as important."

"You can't put your career before your family." The anger in Trey's voice makes Rosie realize that he really might not be talking to her. She remembers his ex-wife, and the dissolution of that marriage.

"Trey, I'm just saying there can be a balance. Don't you think there can be a balance?" He doesn't answer. The TV drones on, their faces turned to it, but neither of them really appears to hear it. Soon enough, the door opens and James and Kelly come in, thanking them and immediately demanding a full report of the past 80 minutes.

Trey and Rosie walk to his car. "Where should we go?" She tries to take his arm but he moves away. She thinks the argument is over, since to her it's just a minor disagreement and one that doesn't need to be resolved right away.

"I think. I think I need a little time to think about this. It's a big issue for me and . . . I just need to think."

"What exactly are you saying?"

"Just that I need to think."

They drive back to Rosie's without saying anything. He leaves her alone, with a hand on the door. She turns back to watch him drive away, unable to react, cracked and falling down, before she can turn the key to unlock the door. She remembers the first time she walked to this door, less than a year ago, and Richard's yellow rain coat in the fog. The street is empty and the lights in the house are out. The breeze rushes by and takes her voice as she says Happy New Year to no one. She walks in and for the first time in a long time wishes the door would somehow lead her somewhere else.

January 2002

Two days go by. She leaves messages for Trey on his cell phone, hoping that he'll call. Pacing, she listens to messages, which she looks for each time she enters her apartment. It's Richard, it's Mom, it's Jess from graduate school, but it's not Trey calling to tell her anything. She finds things to occupy her mind and her body while her heart is flailing. Her bicycle becomes her companion again, more than it has since graduate school, and she pedals over hills to get her blood moving, as if the working of her heart and vessels will squeeze out her disconsolation. Certainly, it will siphon the blood from her mind, rendering it numb. Rosie calls her mother and bursts into tears when she asks about Trey.

She tells her mother of his absence for the last 36 hours, and her mother offers advice and validation, making her feel less alone for a few minutes, then more so once she hangs up and registers the 3,000 mile expanse between her and her family. She had begun to have a new family, and she misses Trey terribly as though half of her self was he. Remembering they didn't know each other a short time ago doesn't help her. She knocks on Richard and Ken's door. They comfort her with a cup of tea and together they take Sammy to the beach. It reminds Rosie of her first meeting on the beach with Trey and her initial excitement. As tears roll down her face Richard reminds her of how fate brought them together that Saturday morning in June, and if he's still on the planet their relationship could still happen. Ken suggests alien abduction. Rosie wipes her face and laughs; a staccato release of emotion. Richard and Ken tell her it's probably old wounds Trey has. Time, they tell her, and she wants to scream. Waiting on time has become like standing in a subway station waiting for a broken down train.

A third day goes by and finally the phone rings. Rosie is shaking as she listens for a response to her hello.

"Hi, Rosie."

"I miss you." She's immediately crying again.

"Me, too. I'm sorry I haven't called. I needed time to think and then . . ." other reasons flash in her mind. Someone else? She imagines a solid woman in an apron who makes her own bread. Instead she hears, "my dad collapsed."

"No! Oh God, when? Where is he? How is he?"

"He's stable. He's in the hospital." Trey sounds weak and she hears him sniffle as he tells her, "He collapsed on New Years day. Rosie, it's bad. He has pancreatic cancer and there's metastatic disease. It looks bad. Mom called the ambulance, then us and I got there as soon as I could. I've been with her and I wanted to call you, but it's been so hard and so intense. When I finally looked at the clock yesterday it was just too late to call. And the way we left things, the way *I* left things--"

"Where are you?"

"At mom and dad's, just getting some stuff for them."

"Stay there. I'm coming." She hangs up, grabs her wallet, and goes. Without thinking she's on her bicycle, and her adrenaline makes the trip almost as short as a car ride.

He opens the door as she's running up the steps. She wraps her arms around him like he's the bud of a flower needing protection, and unable to bloom. She feels him cry in her arms and her heart. She aches to somehow take away some of his pain.

They go in the house and she wants to talk, but knows her time now is to listen. Trey's eyes are red, his shirt looks crooked, he sits with Rosie on the edge of the couch for a few minutes then jumps up when he thinks of something else he has to retrieve. There's a bag in the hallway, and Rosie notices shampoo peeking out and the top of a tube of toothpaste. What can I do? complicates a situation already too taxing for Trey, so instead she asks, "Can I get some clothes together for your mom?" He stops and looks at her and tension slides down from his shoulders as he breathes a sigh to tell her yes.

She's not prepared to see Jim Davids in a hospital bed; the doctor who she followed on rounds through the same halls they now walk. They turn into the room and he's there, in a blue patterned hospital gown, sitting upright in the bed, strings of IVs dangling from his arms.

"Hi Rosie," he smiles and she notices that he actually looks slightly better. The jaundice is not as terrible as she had anticipated, and the fact that he's improved so much from the fluids tells her how dehydrated and malnourished he had been. She checks herself, knowing from Trey's explanation his appearance is deceiving.

"How are you?" She asks after hugging Kate and sitting on one of chairs that have been collected at the side of his bed.

"Not too bad. Better since they put a stent in yesterday."

"Stent?"

"They did a scope. The tumor was preventing my pancreas from functioning properly."

She nods. "I'm sorry. Trey told me the diagnosis and, I'm just so sorry."

He shrugs. "We all knew something was going on. I half expected this." His quiet voice does not reflect the confidence of his statement.

"How long will they keep you here?"

"A few more days. My electrolytes aren't quite there yet. And I'll probably have the first chemo before I go."

The mention of chemo makes Rosie shutter. Though she's been on the hospital floors many times as a student, personal reasons haven't brought her there for several years. She recognizes that even amidst the grief of those in the room now, she may be the least prepared to cope with the coming months.

Kate and Trey launch in to conversation, and he offers her the bag of supplies he and Rosie gathered from the house. Kate's smile is weak, and she looks exhausted. Rosie thinks of the room that Octavius was in, during his final hospital stay, and how his mother had looked at her with as weary an expression, with a smile that really indicated profound sorrow. This time, though, the memory reminds Rosie to think of life, and of quality of life. She's able to don her clinical hat momentarily to ask Jim about pain, plans of care, and prognosis.

"Six months to two years, if things go well."

Rosie blinks hard and breathes deeply. Trey and Kate have ceased their conversation, and Trey stands next to her now. She looks up at him and reaches for his hand. "Well," she begins, turning her gaze back to Jim, "How can we make it so they're the best years, or months and days that you can possibly have?"

Trey brings her home and comes in. They talk about their previous conversation, and Trey admits he had directed his comments to his ex-wife, when he had responded to Rosie's position on motherhood and career. He agrees about balance, but they disagree on the way to achieve it. In the end, they agree to disagree, and leave the topic to be revisited at a later date but not abandoned. Trey stays.

Rosie sleeps deeply. She catches up on the hours of rest lost while waiting for Trey to call, and the work of cycling makes her body require a regenerative rest. She dreams again, of Octavius. This time he's running. There's nothing else. No ground, no backdrop, no surroundings. There's just the sound of his laughter and his feet falling in an ecstatic slow motion sprint, pushing the invisible ground away. As the sun rises she turns to Trey and hugs him to her, feeling him, in his sleep, fall toward her. He begins to awaken and as they meet, she has the oddest sensation that everything will be all right.

The chemotherapy starts. Dr. Davids returns home. On a good day he ventures in to the office. Rosie becomes aware of this outing when her cell phone rings at work, during her lunch break. She recognizes the clinic phone number.

"Rosie, I'm glad I got you. I'd like to arrange a time to speak with you at greater length. Are you with a patient?" She hears fatigue in his voice but also some excitement.

"No, I'm actually at lunch, so I have a little time now. So you couldn't stay away from the office?"

He laughs. "Yeah, I suppose it's a bit of a challenge. Listen, we got the grant."

"Really? That's great!"

"Because of my . . . situation, we're going to have to move rather quickly on this." He begins to explain his plan to transform the clinic. He'll hire a full time manager, offering the position to the part time employee who performs these duties first. The plans include some renovations, involving the purchase of the adjacent office, which will provide for more exam rooms and the office space for a nurse practitioner. As Rosie listens, she grows excited, and calculates the notice she'll have to give at her current position in order to start at the clinic. Dr. Davids explains that he'd like her to start soon, since he will be unable to work and his patients will need continuity of care. It's a fast transition; a transformative growth that eerily parallels the speed that the cancer will likely follow. Rosie composes her letter of resignation after she hangs up the phone.

The next few weeks contain full days, with Rosie traveling to the clinic after work to assist with planning, meeting contractors, discussing carpet color and pattern, countertops, and the size and location of her personal office. The manager takes the reigns for the majority of these tasks, and Dr. Davids assists as much as he can, leaning on Kate's arm as they tour the clinic and visualize the changes. Rosie watches them discuss the renovation, and admires how Jim listens to Kate's input with consideration and immense respect. Rosie and Jim talk about which physicians he will approach to join the practice, and she adds little as Jim rattles through the names of infectious disease and community health fellows. They discuss where to advertise. Rosie reviews HIV care, which has changed only slightly since her clinical rotations. Her work at the clinic will involve treating the homeless, and, if they have HIV, it will be only one of their problems. Dr. Davids has developed a team of providers to assist with health concerns that expand beyond the physical body, and he plans to offer space weekly for the psychologist and case manager to spend time at the clinic. The list of resources that he and his staff have compiled for this population—food, shelter, drug and alcohol recovery, mental health treatment, transportation, pharmaceutical assistance-- is impressive.

The workers hammer out walls as Rosie begins her work there, alone, relying on Margaret, the office nurse for occasional clinical advice when she's uncertain. She thinks aloud to Margaret, who's worked here for fifteen years and will likely retire in another five. The two women are both aware that if Margaret wasn't as close to retiring, she could easily obtain an advanced degree and fill Rosie's position. For this reason, Rosie respects her, and treats her as a peer, delegating phone calls or tasks carefully, and only when she does not have the time to complete them herself. Jim is available on his cell phone, and he comes in once a week to review complicated cases with Rosie. She works closely with the case manager, and patients leave grateful for the assistance they've received.

The interviews for physicians are minimal, since Jim recognizes most of the applicants and weeds through the resumes to select appropriate candidates. They choose Shirley Mason, who will become the part time physician and Kevin Chan, who will work full time. Both doctors are young, ambitious, and dedicated to the population for which the clinic cares. Rosie learns within the first week of working with Shirley that she has two young children, and the devotion she has for both her children and her career gives Rosie a better idea of how family and business can mix. Kevin is married, and over time will complain about how his timeline for having children precedes his wife's.

Rosie's long days lead to some bickering with Trey, and the stress of the family illness escalates some arguments that would have otherwise been minor disputes. To assure him, she plans days to leave work on time to go see him. They sleep in on Saturdays and Sundays, and have dinner with his parents on Sunday nights.

In late March, they work together in her small kitchen to prepare dinner for his family. They play music, chop onions, mince garlic, and Rosie sinks her hands into the ground meat to mix the meatballs. She pushes it around the bowl, mentally noting what she's tried and hasn't, making adjustments that she hopes will be just subtle enough. Trey interrupts her thoughts with a question about the lettuce and she shushes him long enough to add the ground pepper.

"Are you choosing ground pepper over me?" He asks.

"Not a chance," and she hugs him with her wrists flexed.

The pasta boils, the salad is prepared, and the sauce is simmering. The oven clicks on and off as the garlic bread toasts. Trey opens a bottle of Chianti as Rosie opens the door to greet Jim and Kate. They have club soda for Jim. James, Kelly, and Lila join them, as well, and Kelly enters first carrying Lila with James following, holding a tira misu cake from a North Beach bakery. Her table is small but they pull up enough chairs and Lila falls asleep in Kelly's arms while nursing.

The clicking of silverware halts conversation when they begin to eat. The garlic bread and salad are passed around the table.

"These meatballs!" James exclaims.

"Yes," Kate agrees. "They're the best I've ever had."

Trey turns to Rosie. "I think you did it." Rosie smiles and nods excitedly, and picks up her glass to toast Trey. There's laughter and joy at the table, but when Jim excuses himself to lie on the couch, a grey hush descends upon the family. Kate watches him close his eyes. "You okay, honey?" she asks.

"Just resting. I'm alright."

Rosie, Shirley, Kevin, Margaret, and the new nurse Amanda develop a solid working relationship. They learn each other's personality quirks, and take care of each other as they care for the patients. The manager Rosanna keeps the clinic flowing and assists with scheduling when Henry, who works at the front desk is pulled in various directions or needs to take time to get lunch.

In April, Rosie looks up from a chart to see Tommy following Margaret down the hall. He's limping, since his toe was amputated, but he otherwise looks great. Rosie sees right away that he's gained weight and his skin looks healthy. His hair still hangs in a ponytail down his back. She enters the exam room and glances at his vital signs, which are perfect.

"Tommy. It's so good to see you again. How are you?"

"Good! How are you?"

"Good. Glad to be back in the clinic! How's your housing situation?"

"Fine. Good. So what's going on with Dr. Davids?" The question is common amongst the patients, and with some people she elaborates in greater detail about his absence. With Tommy, she feels she can be completely honest, and she puts down the chart to tell him about the diagnosis. Tommy's face seems to crack with worry.

"What does that mean? When is he coming back?"

"I don't think he is, Tommy." She says this softly, watching his response. "He comes in about once a week now, but in terms of practicing . . ." she watches his countenance continue to crumble. "He's not coming back."

"I'm going to really miss him. He saved my life."

"I know. He helped a lot of people."

"You saved my life, too, Rosie. Thank you."

"I'm glad I could help you. That was a pretty scary day for all of us."

"You can say that again! So will I be able to see him? To at least say good bye?"

"Let me talk to him about that, okay?"

They go on to discuss his medication. He has a few side effects of occasional diarrhea and not being able to stay out in the sun for long, but he is otherwise happy with the medicine he takes. The regimen is only a few pills once a day, is easy to remember, and doesn't need to be accompanied by a meal. Rosie orders blood work to make sure the medicine isn't too taxing on his organs, and makes sure he's had a fasting cholesterol check within the past year. They talk about safer sex, and she asks about sobriety.

"Five years sober." He smiles proudly.

"Good for you."

"Yeah."

She calls Kate to speak to Jim about coming in to see Tommy. When Kate hears her voice though, she begins to cry.

"The chemo isn't working. He's had all the options and it's not working. We just got the results of the last CT scan. Everything's worse. It's everywhere." The words ring through Rosie's mind with harsh intensity. That's awful, is all she can think and all she can say, even, knowing that words are terribly inadequate at this moment. "We're thinking . . ." Kate sobs, clears her throat and begins again. "We're thinking this is enough. He's had all the nausea and pain he can take. It's not worth it. It's no quality of life for him. Even though . . ."

"I know. I mean, I don't know everything you're going through, Kate. It's so much. But I think you're right. And you have to make the best decision, even if it means the end of his life." Kate cries, and Rosie tells her with compassion she'll talk to her more at a later time. She tells her good-bye, hangs up, and calls Trey.

That evening, she and Trey wait outside of Richard and Ken's door, waiting for it to open. Richard greets them, and they sit in the living room, not bothering with small talk or comments of how they've set the drapes. Richard knows about Dr. Davids from Rosie and from his reputation in the community.

"I talked to my mom, and they want to proceed with Hospice."

Richard nods. "It's the best choice when you've exhausted everything medical. Especially with pancreatic cancer, where pain is such an issue. We really do a good job with pain management."

"You have nursing staff, round the clock?"

"Yes, in addition to three physicians and a nurse practitioner, who rotate call."

"What kind of room do you have?"

"We're full right now, but I expect that that will change within the next few weeks." It's eerie for Rosie the think that she'll be hoping for someone to die.

"Can you get him a room then?"

"For Dr. Davids? The best room in the house."

"Can will come see him? Can my mother stay with him?"

"We can arrange that."

"How close do your clients need to be?"

"To death, you mean? We usually like to see a doctor's note, or nurse practitioner's note predicting about six months."

"And if they live longer?"

"We don't kick anyone out." Richard smiles kindly. As his smile disappears he adds, softly, "In six months, you won't necessarily want your father to live longer."

Silence. Rosie rubs Trey's back as he rubs his eyes.

Kevin and Rosie ride the community van with Amanda. They focus on their work, yet in the absence of conversation they silently converse. They had pulled away from the clinic after Dr. Davids' last visit. He said good-bye to the staff, the van, and walked the clinic halls, admiring the new space, dragging the tips of his fingers along the wall, once more before he pushed the doors open to exit for the final time. He did not look back. Margaret had ceased speaking to anyone earlier in the week. No one pushed her. The exam rooms, the vials for blood, the samples of drugs, the sound of paper rolls spinning and the crunch and flutter as the table was covered all contained mourning. Patients still filled the waiting room and with relief the providers poured energy and heart into caring for them.

The days that follow involve more sorrow. Trey, James, and Kate gather at the house to help Jim pack for Hospice: a strange gathering of materials for a finite trip. Rosie meets Trey at the end of the day and he relays how horrible the event had been. She listens. She asks concrete questions that he can answer. She cooks him dinner and ignores the heap of food leftover on his plate.

Once Jim has moved into the Hospice house, a cloud somehow lifts. Rosie and Trey go to a movie, a comedy, and they laugh until tears fall down their cheeks. In ensuring Jim's highest quality of care and of life, they somehow increase the quality of the time they spend together, and their lives in general. Their love deepens, widens, and becomes more intricate. The hours they spend together etch patterns in their lives. They immerse in one another.

On a warm Sunday, they walk along the beach where they had first seen each other, almost a year ago. They stop and sit on a bench facing the water and the Golden Gate Bridge. Trey takes her hand, inspecting it.

"What are you looking at?" she can't help but laugh at the slightly odd behavior.

"Rosie," he sighs. "My family is really important to me. They've always been there for me, sharing my disappointments as well as my happiness."

"I know. You have a special bond, all of you."

"I don't know how to ask you this, because I'm asking for a lot." He looks at her and she waits for him to continue. "My father thinks the world of you. He has for a long time, and I think from the first time that he tried to set us up he wanted to see us together. For awhile, I've been feeling the same way, despite all of the stuff going on."

"Uh huh." Rosie's not sure if he's going where she thinks he's going.

"Rosie, I want you to know that what I'm asking you has only a little to do with my father but everything to do with me and what I want. I want you to know that."

"So your question is . . .?"

"Rosie, I'd like us to get married."

Her first reaction is disappointment. Where is the top of the mountain, the horns, the dozen roses, the brilliant diamond ring, the down-on-one-knee? But her mind quickly shifts to the reality of the moment, from the sober downward slide of Jim's health to the beauty all around her, the question in Trey's eyes that she's fallen deeply into and her spiral into love. She puts her hand against his face and kisses him. "I'll marry you." They smile. "But could you just do one thing for me?"

"Sure."

"Could you just, kind of, make that a question, and maybe get on one knee and stuff?"

To her surprise he quickly slides off the bench and props himself on one knee. "Sorry," and he reaches in to a pocket to pull out a ring for her that he offers up, asking, "Domenica Rose Petroni, will you marry me?"

She melts, nods, and lets him slip the ring on her finger. The band is too big and the stone slides down. She turns it to look at the sapphire and diamonds in an antique setting. "It's beautiful," she tells him.

"When we prepared dad for Hospice, he gave me this ring. It's funny, he gave one to James to give to Kelly, but he never offered one when I was married before. It always kind of irked me. Anyway, it was my grandmother's. He told me, 'give it to Rosie, when you're ready.' I decided I was ready."

She kisses him again, through tears. "I'm ready, too."

"I have to ask you for something else." He says seriously. He explains to her how important his father's presence has been to him in all the major events of his life. The sports events, graduations, performances however how small, and how he'd look for his father in the group of onlookers and always feel reassured by his presence. He tells her, "I'm asking you this now because I'd like us to get married, before he dies. I'd like him to see our ceremony, somehow. I'd like him to be there, for me, for us, and for him."

Rosie nods, digesting what this information means. She leans against the bench and looks at the sky, a combination of blue and white. It *is* a lot that he asks. She thinks of the large weddings her cousins have had, in Catholic churches romantically adorned with flowers that the bride walked through in a long white gown. She's always looked on with envy, resolving the emotion with her own assurance to herself that she would one day have her turn. Thinking of Jim, the notion feels childish, and selfish, but she can't shake it. She turns to Trey.

"I'm not opposed to the idea. It's just that I always envisioned something large and elaborate for my wedding, you know?" He looks hurt, so she adds, "I just have to get used to the idea, is all. Really."

"Rosie, I've been married before. And I want to tell you that, from my experience, your wedding day will be miniscule when it comes to what marriage is. I'm not saying the day doesn't matter, and that you shouldn't get everything you dream of—you should. But marriage is much bigger than the ceremony of a wedding."

She thinks about this, squinting her eyes as the sun slants toward them. "Sort of how a life is bigger than the death that ends it."

"Yeah. But . . . backwards." They sit quietly letting this idea sink in.

"Okay," she says finally. "But I want to have my parents there. God, my mother's going to have a fit. We can get married here, in San Francisco. That will be a lot easier on your dad. Do you think--?" She trails off as her imagination continues, molded by Jim's increasing immobility.

"What?"

"I was just thinking, the gardens are so pretty at the Hospice. It would be sort of an unusual setting, but do you think Richard might let us get married there?"

"Hm. It's a thought. It would be easiest for Dad." He puts his arm around her and hugs her to him. "I love you."

Richard's response is one of skepticism. Rosie watches his face as she explains the importance, the promise to keep the ceremony small, quick, and unpretentious. He listens, nodding, shifting his weight, clearing his throat, and finally agreeing as he bear hugs her, lifting her off her feet and shouting, "Congratulations!" Ken smiles and hugs her as well, but not as elaborately.

Her mother is aghast, although her initial response at the news of the engagement is elation. "John!! Rosie's engaged to be married!" Her father takes the phone and congratulates her. There's a pause as she hears him hand it back to her mother.

"You know, long engagements are popular these days. Do you have a date?"

"We're actually planning on having a wedding very soon. Like, in three weeks."

"Three weeks! Honey, are you pregnant?"

"No, no, no." She explains Jim's situation, and both of her parents are saddened by the news.

"Well, if we get invitations out right away, maybe . . ."

"Mom, we actually want to have something very small."

"But your Aunt Mary—"

"I know, but this is important." She explains the ideal of having just their immediate family in the grounds of the Hospice.

"You're going to get married at a morgue?"

"No, Mom. A Hospice."

"But people are dead there, right?"

"No, Mom, they're not dead. Just dying."

"Hm."

"You know, we're all dying if you think about it."

"John!!! Rosie wants to get married at a morgue!" Rosie holds the phone away from her, closes her eyes, and takes a deep breath.

A week before their wedding, they visit the Hospice. Rosie enters Jim's room and sees someone sitting in a chair next to his bed, recognizing immediately the long ponytail and slightly hunched shoulders. He seems luminescent as the light from the window frames his figure. He turns when he sees Jim look at her.

"Hi Tommy."

"Hey, Rosie." Trey steps in behind her.

"Tommy, this is my son, Trey." Rosie blushes as a knowing look passes over Tommy's face when he looks from her to Trey. "Good to meet you."

"Same here." They shake hands. Silence follows. Rosie shifts her weight. Jim closes his eyes.

"Well, I should get going." Tommy stands up.

"You don't have to go—"

"No, I do. I've been bothering Doc for long enough."

"No bother." He reaches a hand toward Tommy.

"Thanks, Doc. Guess I'll see you around."

"You bet."

Tommy leaves and Trey looks at his father. "A patient?"

Jim nods. "Probably breaches patient provider boundaries, but at this point, who gives a fuck, right?" She startles at his language.

Trey sighs and takes the seat next to the bed. "You're right, Dad." It occurs to Rosie that every one she's seen with cancer exhibits anger. She realizes why as she looks at Jim's gaunt and yellow face. The vehicle of his body disintegrates but his mind rages on.

The fog rolls in early on the afternoon of their wedding. As agreed, the ceremony is brief. Jim sits in a wheelchair, attentive and smiling, and Kate stands next to him in a modest but formal dress with her hand on his shoulder. Rosie's parents have succumbed to the idea rather than agreed with vigor, but they shower the couple with love and good wishes. A few others clients are their guests, enjoying the happy event as a welcome change of routine.

Rosie's dress is white, modest, and still flattering. Trey holds her hand and wears a dark suit. Sammy has been invited, and she sits at Ken's feet, eyeing the people with unfamiliar smell from the other side of his legs. The hospice is familiar to her, since Richard often brings her to work to perform her dog-therapy rounds. There's a cluster of chairs, and the guests watch as Rosie and Trey repeat their vows. A light rain begins to fall, and they hurry indoors, helping the clients where needed, then plan transportation to the restaurant where they will celebrate. Jim congratulates them and excuses himself to return to his room, and Trey watches somberly as Kate pushes him down the hall. It's a bittersweet moment for Rosie, as well, and she squeezes his hand with understanding.

They drive south for a honeymoon, taking a long weekend to stay by the ocean. They drive inland to visit vineyards and return to dine at restaurants that overlook the ocean. They eat well, relax, and enjoy being together. On the third morning, Rosie wakes before Trey, and quietly dresses to go for a walk by the water. The sun is just up, and the sky morphs into various shades of color. Rosie finds a piece of driftwood and sits down.

"Rosie Davids," she murmurs out loud, and smiles to herself. She hugs her knees, since the morning hasn't yet wrung out the chill of the night. The water rolls in on itself nonchalantly, and she hypnotically watches it, beginning to breathe with the waves. She thinks of the miles and events that have lead to this point in her life, shuddering with the memory of times of which she's ashamed; the miscalculated relationships, the patients she wishes she'd done something different for, and her immaturity in coping with Octavius' illness and then death. The memories bring on others, and they spin and circle until she orders them to stop. The silence of absent thought ensues. A water bird hurries back from a wave. She thinks of Trey. She thinks of love. She looks across the water and feels the future. Her life can be a gift, a blessing, an instrument for healing. Her thoughts turn to her marriage. They've looked at a few houses together. The clinic runs as if it has an independent heart and will. Things, she realizes, are good. Still, she's haunted by the image of Kate pushing Jim down the Hospice hall. Except for cancer, things are good. She stands, brushes the sand from her legs, and turns to walk back.

When she quietly re-enters their room, she notices Trey's cell phone lit up on the kitchen counter. She reaches it just as the vibrating hum ceases, but in time to see that it's Kate who has called. The clock reads 7:00am, too early for Kate to call with good news. Bracing, she gently wakes Trey to tell him. He sits up, looks at her for a long moment, and gets up to call his mother.

In a frenzied blur she hurls things into bags as Trey trips over his jeans getting into them. She won't recall these moments of packing, the choppy words they toss back and forth regarding the details of their abrupt leaving. But there's a moment, with her hand on the door, when she looks at the disheveled room, eyeing it from one end to the other, when her mind snaps a picture. The moments of happiness etch in even through this horrible reason for leaving. The blue pattern of the bedspread, the throw rugs woven in shades of blue, the cream colored drapery and the coffee pot still laden with brew. The morning light through the window stretches fingertips across the bed. She pulls the door closed and they are gone.

The sound of traffic engulfs them and the scenery blurs by. Rosie drives, glancing over at Trey periodically, and touches his leg. He wipes the side on his face, squeezes her hand briefly and lets go. He's looking ahead at the road and doesn't turn to face her.

Jim had died at night. Like Rosie, Kate had awoken at dawn and peered at him from the other side of the room, where she slept on a cot. She'd watched, stared, squinted as her eyes began to dry then tear, then hurried across the room to place a hand on his chest. The body was cold and still, and she had knelt by it, quietly sobbing, until her knees ached and she realized time would only go forward.

When Trey and Rosie arrive, Richard is at the Hospice. The body is still in the room. Kate and James are in the sitting room, and Rosie can see the curving hunch of Kate, shuddering, clinging to a tissue, as James sits across from her, leaning toward her and bowing his head. Rosie walks behind Trey as Richard opens the door for him. He doesn't turn from the face, the cachetic remains of the shell his father inhabited. The shades are mostly drawn, with the morning light cracking in where they almost touch. Trey's steps are long and slow as he approaches the bed. He stands for a moment, looking, and Rosie touches the back of his arm, stiff at his side. Trey cries as he utters, "Bye, Dad." Tears fall from the corners of Rosie's eyes as she stutters an awkward good-bye. Jim's body has the odd appearance of life at a distance but complete inanimate chill up close. Richard ushers them out, knowing what to say, how to move, when to gently touch the family members to direct them on where to go and what to do next. He's able to draw Kate out, allowing her to feel but maintain her grounding when he discusses the death and confirms the plan for cremation. Kelly is here now, swaying in the corner of the room with Lila, who wiggles in her mother's arms, smiling. Through tears, Kate looks at the baby, wipes the corners of her eyes, and sighs, closing them slowly as the corners of her mouth turn up slightly for a moment, then collapse once again into grief.

The following Saturday, they gather on the bluff overlooking the Pacific Ocean. A small crowd has gathered. Rosie looks around as they wait for the ceremony to begin with the rising sun. The breeze blows and the waves heave in and out. The light is surreal, making even the familiar faces almost unrecognizable. Jim's sister favors her brother, and stands with her husband and grown children next to Kate. James, Kelly, Trey and Rosie flank her other side, and they stand as if blocking the wind, protecting her from the elements, as if they could block the strongest force of grief clearly rising from within her. There are a few cousins, an elderly aunt and uncle. Everyone dresses in black. Several friends arrive, wandering in, shuffling about in an attempt to find a suitable spot, and speaking in quiet tones. Behind them, Rosie sees a familiar group of faces, and recognizes Tommy amongst them. The ceremony was meant to be small, just family and a few close friends, but Margaret had leaked word to a patient, and the information spread quickly through the small community. Tommy stands with his fingers interwoven, rocking forward and back from heel to toe unevenly, squeezing his eyes open and shut, watching the water. Rosie looks at him for a long moment, willing him to meet her gaze. But he continues staring across the water, as if something might appear on the deep blue horizon, as if there's somewhere else to go.

Rosie looks down. The sandy earth blurs as memory fills her mind's eye. She sees the floorboards of Dr. Davids' car. They lay below her feet: light brown, dusted with sand, matted, scattered with a few leaves. The street lights change one by one to green and she looks at him when he utters his partial thoughts out loud. Afraid to ask him to repeat himself, she looks back at the street ahead of them. She feels cold and hot at the same time, shivering yet adjusting the sleeves of her shirt as sweat soaks into the creases. When she turns to look at him, his face is full, almost round, and his eyes are wide open, awake and alive. Now, on the bluff, she shifts her gaze, looking at the water, back at the crowd, but she's pulled back to the memory; half running to keep up with him, her lab coat trailing behind her, as he strides quickly through the halls of the hospital, following his motions as she scrubs in, holding her hands up just as he does after pulling down her surgical mask, standing where he indicates, and she sees, as if he is here, his face in the recovery room when he smiles at her and tells her she's done well. His cheeks creased with age, pink with life, eyes slightly tired but rimmed with the light of relief. She looks at the urn and feels the hollow void of grief. It comes sudden and fierce, and she shifts her weight several times and swallows hard. Trey is absorbed in his aunt's words as she addresses the crowd. Rosie looks around, startled, when she meets Tommy's gaze. She recalls how pale he looked that day that seems like years ago. Their eyes lock for several moments and simultaneously they turn away.

When the movement of air pauses to let the sun stretch forth across the morning, Kate, James, Trey, and Jim's sister, take handfuls of ash and lovingly cast it toward the water. There are last words, thoughts, wishes, as the union of the crowd dissipates, and people begin to turn in odd directions to disengage from one another. As Jim's ashes float away, there's nothing more to hold this collection of people together.

Rosie hugs Trey. He goes to put his arms around his mother and Rosie walks to Tommy.

"Hi, Rosie."

"Hey Tommy."

"I can't believe he's gone." She nods. "I hate it that he's gone."

"You were important to him." He stares across the water. His brows are furrowed. His eyes are red. "I'm sorry, Tommy, I just . . .. I don't know what to say." Realizing this, she stops.

"He changed my life. I was at the bottom of the bottom when I met him, and he showed me the way. He showed me that I could be healthy. That I deserved to be alive. He just . . . believed in me."

She watches the tears roll down his cheeks. "Tommy." She touches his arm. He glances at her, then again his eyes turn to the distance. "I hate it that he's gone, too. He was a wonderful and amazing person. But Tommy, you deserve to be alive. You deserve to be healthy. That doesn't change. He gave you that not to borrow but to keep inside of you. As a tool to heal from all the rotten stuff you had to go through."

Tommy smiles and his face changes as if it were cracking open. He nods and wipes his face with both hands. "You sound like him, you know. Not exactly, but that's sort of what he'd say. The 'strength inside.' It sounds like him."

"You have that strength inside. That's what enabled you to get your life together."

"But it's so . . ." he begins to cry and his voice breaks as his says, "it could fall apart any time. He was such a rock for me."

"I know. And you're right. It could. Life doesn't make a lot of sense and things that happen often don't seem to have a lot of reason behind them." She stops and looks with him into space. "But you'll have other rocks. If you think about it, you probably already do. But Tommy, keep his life inside of you. Keep the memory of him alive in you, not his death, not," she gestures around her, "this."

Trey walks over and shakes his hand. "Tommy, right? Thanks for coming."

"Thank you. I know this is supposed to be just family—"

"You're family. He would have wanted you here."

There are only a few people left, and Tommy turns to go as well. The immediate family gathers to orchestrate their transport to Kate's house. The wind has begun to pick up. Rosie stares into the sea.

"Rosie?" Trey is saying, moving in front of her to stop her stare. She looks at him and focuses on his words. "You ready?"

"Yeah." She breathes in deeply, takes his hand, and turns eastward, feeling the muscle, bone, and strength of his grip and in her own movement. Just before she closes the car door, a large diesel truck slows at the intersection to turn right up Sloat Boulevard, then exudes a plume of dark smoke as the engine heaves it into motion. The smell sends Rosie back to the developing world, as it always does. The car door kisses closed.

Diesel was all that was burnt in Western Africa. Diesel and smoke that lingered in the air because something was always burning: diesel, trash, coal. The fumes hung in the air, made her gag, and stuck to her skin and inside her nostrils. She'd scratch her neck at the end of the day and look at the black underneath her nails when she pulled her hand away. As often as they could, they walked the path to school to avoid some of that filth. The grass would still be wet with dew, but looking at the crowd stuffing itself onto the bus made wet ankles a pleasure. The hem of her skirt would dry by mid-morning, and the students wouldn't notice. It was unusual for her to get to their meeting spot first, but before she could wonder, there he would be, jogging down the hill with his thumbs tucked under the straps of his backpack. Each step became a leap and she smiled at the site of him prancing toward her. His energy seemed inexhaustible.

"Ready?" he said, stopping at her side.

"Yeah. Looking forward to the walk, actually."

"Me, too."

"Really? I couldn't tell," she nudged him with her elbow.

"Come on, then." He began to walk as he said, "and I'll ignore the sarcasm."

He led the way to the path and they stepped off the street between the bar and the store unto the dirt. They both breathed a little harder as the trail turned up a hill, but not so hard as to make conversation impossible.

"Thanks for your advice on Al."

"No problem. Some of these kids are tough to manage."

"I'm not looking forward to trying to manage him today."

"Eh-eh," he turned slightly to shake a finger at her. "Omit 'try' from your vocabulary. You either do or you don't."

"Well, I'm not looking forward to it." A few steps went by in silence. "It's like I told you last night, he has this potential that's obvious but he will not—" she paused.

"You were going to say it weren't you."

"Yes," she groaned.

"It's a disconnect, Rosie. You know, not everything in life makes sense. Not everything that happens matches up or fits neatly into perfect little packages." They reached the end of the rise and he stopped to look around at the view. "Like ice cream . . . in January," he said dreamily.

"Hunh?"

He looked at her quickly, smiled, and looked again at the scene before them. Children walking, jabbering, and chasing each other in their blue and white uniforms could be seen trickling in from all directions. They could see a few point to Octavius, shrieking with delight as they changed direction to veer toward him. Distracted, his voice trailed off: "Too cold for the weather."

As they pull away, she feels the ocean within her, tumbling around, pulsating, tossing away rocks and other salty water debris. When she licks her lips, she can taste it.

It's an odd morning. The tilt of the earth, the season, changes in the sky. Sea gulls bend on the breeze. Gravel rolls under the wheels of the car then stops when they do, as they sit, quietly looking forward, waiting for the light to change.

About the Author

Sarah Kressy Giliberti began working in health care in 1995, when she was employed at Tufts School of Medicine as an assistant project coordinator for an HIV and nutrition research project. She became certified as a nurse practitioner in 2000, and has worked in internal medicine and HIV care since that time. She lives in lower Alabama with her husband and son. This is her first novel.